DATE DUE

Wonder Tales of
Dogs and Cats

Books by Frances Carpenter

by Frances Carpenter

Wonder Tales of Dogs

and Cats

Illustrated by Ezra Jack Keats

Doubleday & Company, Inc., Garden City, New York

This book is dedicated

to

all the dogs and cats I have loved

and especially to Timmy

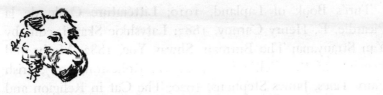

Acknowledgment

The popular folk tales which have been adapted in this book by the author have been collected from many sources. Among these special mention should be made of the following:

Turi's Book of Lapland, 1910; Littérature Orale de la Picardie, E. Henry Carnoy, 1883; Latyshkie Skazki, edit. by Yan Strauyana; The Burman, Shway Yoe, 1882; Myths and Legends of the Celtic Race, T. W. Rolleston, 1927; Irish Fairy Tales, James Stephens, 1920; The Cat in Religion and Magic, Howey; Contes Populaires de Soudan Egyptien, 1909; Savage Childhood, Dudley Kidd, 1906; Contes Populaires d'Afrique, René Basset, 1883; Among the Mongols, James Gilmour; Cabinet of Curiosities, Mémoires sur les Duels, J. Scaliger, 1836; Myths and Legends of Japan, F. Headland Davis, 1912; Japanese Fairy Tales Series, No. 4, Konumsha, Minami Saegicho; Tales of Old Japan, A. B. Mitford, 1886; Les Traditions Populaires de l'Asie Mineur, Carnoy et Nicolaides, 1889, Folk Tales of Kashmir, Rev. J. Hinton Knowles, 1893; South Mountain Magic, M. V. Dahlgren, 1882; Littérature Orale de la Basse Normande, J. Fleury, 1883; Bannu, S. S. Thorburn, 1876; Serbian Folklore, Elodie L. Mijatovich, Rev. W. Denton, 1899; Contes Populaires de Basse Bretagne, F. M. Luzel, 1887.

Contents

CONTENTS

CONTENTS

CONTENTS

Wonder Tales of Dogs and Cats

Dog Luck

Inside the round reindeer-skin tent, it was cozy and warm.
The fire on the ground was burning high. Huka, the Lapp
boy, thought the flames were trying to leap up through the
smoke hole over his head.

Outside, the snow was falling and falling. Icy winds blew
across the bleak northern land. Whistling and howling, they
shook the stiff sides of the skin tent.

The Lapp family inside that reindeer-skin tent did not
seem to mind the storm. In the light of the fire, their tanned
faces shone, happy and smiling. And they were talking and
talking.

"A day to remember is this!" said Nilas, the father.

"A day of 'dog luck' it is," said Elle, the mother.

The man and the woman were comfortably settled on the
sitting-log by the fire. Their children were squatting near,
on the twig-covered ground. And in the best place of all that
night, closest to the fire, lay Kako, the dog.

Three dogs lived in the tent with this Lapp family. But

15

that night it was only one, Kako, whose head the children were patting. It was only of Kako that people were talking. It was about the dog, Kako, that Huka was singing, in the Lapp fashion.

"Voya, voya! Nana, nana!
    Kako is a good dog!

"Voya, voya! Nana, nana!
    Kako is a brave dog!

"Voya, voya! Nana, nana!
    Kako is the best dog
    Of all dogs, everywhere!

"Oh, Mother, feed this good dog
    Who is not afraid of the wolves."

It had all happened that afternoon when Nilas and his son, Huka, were out on their skis with the reindeer. Over and over, the story now had been told. How Nilas had been driving the reindeer! How the three dogs had been helping, running after the deer and nipping their feet! And how, all at once, the wolves had come dashing out of the woods!

Nilas and Huka had shouted and shouted to frighten the wolves. The dogs had barked and barked, as good reindeer dogs should. At the sound of the shouting and barking, the wolves had run away.

That is, all but one wolf had run away. And that one was the biggest wolf Huka ever had seen.

The great beast made straight for the boy's father. Snapping and snarling, it sent the dogs flying out of its way.

16

Oh, that wolf was quick! Try as he might, the Lapp could not land one blow of his ski pole on the beast's head.

And that wolf was bold. Closer and closer it came. It came so close at last that it caught one of the man's skis between its great teeth.

That wolf was strong too. With a mighty pull, it tore the wood ski right off the man's foot. Nilas was thrown down flat on the snow. At once the wolf was upon him.

Luckily Kako had come back to help his master. Just in time, the brave dog jumped on the wolf. Kako's sharp teeth bit deep, deep into the back of the beast. With a wild scream of pain, the wolf shook the dog off, and ran away over the snow.

So it was the dog, Kako, who saved his master's life. Everyone said so, there beside the blazing fire.

"Aye, a brave dog is our Kako," the Lapp herder said to his children. "A fierce dog he is, fierce as any wolf."

"Is it true, Father, that dogs once were wolves themselves?" Huka asked, as he threw another bone to the dog hero.

"How could I know?" Nilas answered the boy. "It must have been long, long ago. And I was not there."

"Some people do say the dog once was a wolf," the Lapp father said thoughtfully. "But some say, instead, the dog once was a fox. Everyone says the dog once was a wild creature. He had the same shaggy coat, the same long waving tail, and the same pointed nose which a dog has today. But

17

he was wild, wild. It was a long, long time before that wild dog-creature learned to be a true dog and live in the tents with the people."

"My own grandfather was a wise man, my children," Nilas was remembering. "My grandfather always spoke truly. And he said this is the true story of how the dog became a dog."

In the beginning, when the world was new, the wild dog-creature ran through the deep woods, hunting his food. He slept under leaves, or behind a rock, or in a cave. Often he was cold, so cold he almost froze to death. Often he was hungry. Oh, yes, the wild dog was hungry often enough.

Then, as now, big beasts ate little beasts. Fierce beasts ate timid beasts. And that is why the gentle reindeer was so often the food of the wolves and the bears, and the wild dogs as well.

Where there were many deer, there was food for all the wild beasts. Let a reindeer fall to the ground, and at once there came wolves, foxes and bears, and wild dogs too. All would eat their fill of the good deer meat.

But if there were not many reindeer? Then it was quite another story. Let the wolves find a deer at last, and they would not let any other hungry creature come near.

Now, in those days, too, there were Lapps in this land. Even in the very beginning, the Lapps were here.

The Lapps, like the wild beasts, ate the reindeer. Reindeer meat was their best food. Reindeer milk made their cheese. And reindeer skins could be used for clothes and for tents.

So the Lapps gathered up the reindeer into herds. And they kept watch, then as now, lest wolves should come near them.

Most of the beasts were afraid of these men with their long ski poles. Men had sharp knives. The beasts tried to keep well out of reach of these ski poles and knives.

Perhaps the wild dog was not quite so afraid as other beasts were. Or perhaps he was more curious about the ways of men. He often crept close to watch the Lapp herders tending their deer.

"So many, many reindeer!" one wild dog thought as he watched. "No dog would ever be hungry if he lived with such a man."

"Suppose I should go to live with that one," the wild dog said to himself. He was watching a Lapp gather his reindeer together. The man was running this way and that way after his deer.

"I could run faster than he does," the dog said to himself. "I could nip the feet of the reindeer. I could make them go where he wants them to go."

The dog heard the man shouting and shouting to scare off the wolves. His shouts were loud and sharp. They sounded almost like a dog barking.

"I could bark ever so much louder than he does," the dog said again to himself.

Slowly the wild dog crept toward the man. At first the

19

Lapp thought the dog wanted to eat the deer. He was starting to swing his long ski pole when the dog spoke aloud.

Hearing a beast speak did not surprise this Lapp. In the beginning, people say, all animals could speak—and rocks and trees, too.

Animals still talk today. Of that we may be sure. Animals can understand men, but men can no longer understand the beasts. Why this should be so, I do not know. Our times are different from those ancient times.

But the Lapp was surprised at what the dog said to him. "I have come to help you gather your reindeer together," the dog said to the man. "I do not come to eat them." And that dog ran around and around the man's herd. He drove the timid reindeer this way and that way, just where the man wished. And the man was pleased.

"This is good," the Lapp said to the wild dog. "I need someone like you to help me with the deer. Work for me, and I will give you a place in my tent. You shall warm yourself by my fire. You shall eat my good reindeer soup. In return you shall keep watch for the wolves. You shall bark when any strange man or beast comes near our tent."

"Well, I will try it," the wild dog agreed. Secretly he was afraid of this man. Too many beasts he knew had been killed by such as he.

But it was warm inside the Lapp tent. It was good to lie by the fire. The dog liked the reindeer soup out of the Lapp's cooking pot. He liked to play with the Lapp's children.

Still the wild dog was afraid. Each time the man picked

20

up his sharp knife, the animal trembled. He was so afraid that the hair stood up on end along his back.

And after a few days, the wild dog ran back to the deep woods. You see, it was not easy at first for this wild creature to learn how to be a dog.

That was a terrible winter. Reindeer—wild reindeer—were hard to come upon. The dog always was hungry.

In one place he found the bones of a rabbit. But the bones were bare of meat.

In another place he dug the bones of a fox out of the snow. But only the furry foxtail was left.

Once he smelled fresh deer meat. He ran fast, very fast. But he got there too late. Around the fallen reindeer there was already a crowd of fierce, hungry wolves. So many were there that the starving dog could not snatch even one tiny bone.

The next bones he found were those of a wild dog, just like himself. "Oh, oh!" the dog cried. "These might be my own bones. Soon it will be me the wolves will be eating. I am safer, by far, in the tent of the Lapp." And, as fast as ever he could, he ran over the snow to find his former master.

"I will stay with you forever," the wild dog said to the man. "I will work for you well if you will promise never to lift your ski pole against me and never to hurt me with your sharp knife."

"I promise," said the man. "Dog and man, we shall work together. And always and always we shall be friends."

In time, the wild dog-creature learned to be a true dog. Each day he drove the reindeer for the Lapp. Soon he could bring them home by himself. Even far, far away he could smell the wolf smell. Always he barked for his master in time. None of that Lapp's deer were lost after the dog came to stay in his tent.

The Lapp's herd grew larger and larger. So many deer did he have at last, that he needed more dogs to help him.

"Go into the deep woods," the Lapp said one day to his four-footed helper. "Bring back your brothers to work for me too."

"I will go," said the dog. "I will tell them just how it is to live in the tents. Perhaps they will come."

The wild dogs were surprised to see their lost brother. They thought he had long ago been eaten by wolves. But here he stood before them, fat and well fed. They themselves were thin, just skin and bones, after their hungry winter.

"It is good to live in the tents," the dog said to his wild brothers. "Each night I sleep warm. I have all I can eat. And my master is my friend."

When they heard this, those wild dogs thought they, too, would like to work for the Lapps. More and more came, until there were dogs by the fire in every tent.

Men found out that if they were kind to their dogs their herds grew big. Their luck was good. "Dog luck" they called it. They wished for "dog luck" with their reindeer here on

22

the earth. And they hoped for "dog luck" in heaven later on when they died.

"In Heaven, once again, dogs will be heard." Nilas ended the story. "They will tell God Himself whether or not their masters treated them well. It would be bad for any man there if his dog said that his master had beaten him. It would be bad, too, if he told God he had not had enough reindeer soup after the day's work. But, of course, only a man with an ungrateful heart would be unkind to such a good friend as his dog."

The Kingdom
without a Cat

Neighbors often came to spend the evening in the farm-house kitchen of Pierre Dumont. The men liked to play cards with this merry farmer. The women liked to bring their knitting and talk with his good wife. And one and all liked the stories that were told by this French farmer's old mother, from her seat by the stove.

One evening all the neighbors were there. Madame Dumont was spinning. Knitting needles were flying. Cards were being played.

No one was idle except the big gray cat, curled up at the feet of old Grandmother Dumont. That big gray cat lay there, quite still, not even purring.

"Look at the lazy one!" One of the men pointed his pipe at the sleeping cat. "Ho, a cat's life is the good life. Plenty of milk to drink, and all day to sleep!"

"But no, my friend," said Grandmother Dumont, putting her sewing down in her lap. "Our cat is not lazy. No cat

25

in this village works harder. Seven mice and two rats has this cat killed today. He is as good at his cat's work as the cat in a story my old granny once told me."

The old woman was thinking about a very old tale. She called it "The Tale of the Kingdom without a Cat." As she began to tell it that night, the card game was forgotten. The spinning wheel and the knitting needles all moved more slowly. And just as she told it then to her neighbors, I set the tale down here for you.

In this land of France there once lived a poor miller with his wife and three sons. When they were young, the miller and his family were comfortable enough in the little stone mill. They had a sturdy donkey to turn the millstone around. And farmers from near and far paid them well to grind grain for them.

The neighbors said this miller and his good wife spoiled their two older sons. No one ever saw those two lazy boys working. It was always the youngest one, Jean, who was called on to help in that mill.

But when the miller and his good wife grew old, it was a different matter. First the boys' mother died. Then their old father fell ill. There was no one to run the mill but the three brothers. But even then it was Jean, the miller's youngest son, who did most of the work.

One day the miller called his three sons together about his bed.

"My time is near. I am not long for this world. I wish I

had gold to leave to you, my sons. But there is only this mill, and it belongs to the lord of this valley. He will let you live on here, I am sure, so long as you use his mill well. Paul is the oldest. So I must leave the mill to him."

"What do you leave for me, my father?" asked Louis, the second son.

"There is only our donkey. I leave you our good donkey, Louis, my son. Feed him and care for him and he will turn the mill for you. Paul, in charge of the mill, and you, with the donkey, can earn a good living for yourselves and your brother. Take good care of Jean, my sons. Older brothers should always look out for the younger ones. And may Heaven bless you!"

"Is there nothing at all for me then, my father?" the miller's youngest son asked.

"Alas, my dear Jean," the miller said sadly, "there is only Minay, our cat. I do not know what good Minay ever will be to you. But she is all I can leave you." Then, with a great sigh, the poor miller turned his face to the wall and drew his last breath.

Well, it did not turn out at all as the poor miller had hoped. Paul and Louis, selfish fellows, took no care at all of their younger brother, Jean. Instead, they soon put him out of the mill.

"There is no more bread in this house than we need for our own stomachs," they declared. "We are not going to work ourselves to death to feed a great fellow like you. You are young. You are strong. Go find work somewhere else. And take your cat along with you."

Poor Jean picked up the cat in his arms. His tears fell on her fur as he walked away from his old home.

"What shall we do, Minay?" the young fellow cried. "Whatever shall we do now?"

"We shall go forth into the wide world to find our fortune, my master," the wise cat, Minay, said. She rubbed her soft head against the sad young man's shoulder, and he felt better.

Jean and his cat walked all over France. Sometimes a kind farmer's wife gave the young man bread for himself and milk for his cat. But they did not find their fortune until they came at last to a certain kingdom in a far part of the land.

There they found a fine palace that belonged to the King. Its white towers reached high into the blue sky. There were gardens all about it. And it was in a garden that the young man and his cat saw a strange sight.

Finely dressed noblemen were running this way and that way at the foot of the palace steps. Many, many nobles there were, young ones and old ones. Each one had a club with which he was hitting the ground.

"What are those men doing, Minay?" Jean said to the cat. He lifted the animal high up onto his shoulder so that she, too, might see the strange sight he saw.

"It is mice they are after," Minay said to her master. "All those foolish fellows are trying to kill little mice with

28

clubs big enough to kill a great bear. Ha-ha! Ho-ho!" the cat burst out laughing.

Jean began to laugh too. It was a funny sight to see one little mouse with ten grown men running after it. All ten struck at that one little mouse with their ten great clubs.

Jean's sides fairly ached, he laughed so hard. For, of course, the mouse could run faster than those clumsy men. And the mouse was so small that their great clubs never could find it.

The mice were laughing too. They were enjoying this game. Jean saw two of the mice playing tag with each other between the feet of one fat nobleman.

In and out the mice ran, around and around him, not the least bit afraid. The fat man's red face grew redder with every foolish blow of his club. He grew more and more angry. He hit the ground harder and harder.

Jean and the cat laughed louder and louder. "Ha-ha! Ho-ho!"

"You would not laugh if you were in my place, Young Stranger," the fat nobleman cried.

"Why would I not laugh?" Jean replied. "If I acted as you act, it would be just as funny."

"Well, you would not laugh if the King had set you to killing these wicked pests. Our kingdom is full of them. Every man in this palace has been ordered to run after them. But only four mice have we killed in twelve months running."

30

"It would be no trouble at all for us to kill mice. Here, we will show you."

Jean let his cat, Minay, jump out of his arms onto the ground. With one bound, Minay caught the mouse in her mouth. The good cat straightway laid the dead mouse down at the feet of the panting nobleman.

The noble's eyes opened wide. His mouth opened wide, too. He was filled with amazement, and he cried to the others, "Come! Oh, come see this marvel!"

At first Jean could not believe that these men never had seen a cat. He had not thought that, in all the world, there was a country without a cat.

But it was so in this kingdom. The people were as astonished at the sight of a cat killing a mouse, as if the very sun had dropped down out of the sky.

"What magic beast is this?" they all asked at once.

"It is only a cat," Jean replied, smiling.

"A cat? But what is a cat? So much smaller than a man, yet it can kill a mouse, which men cannot do!" they cried out in wonder. Then someone shouted.

"Take care! Take care! This fierce little beast might perhaps kill a man, too."

Jean laughed again. It was funny, indeed, to think of his gentle Minay fiercely killing a man.

"Oh no, my friends. A cat only kills mice. My cat could easily kill all the mice in this kingdom, but never, no, never would she harm a man."

"This magic beast is something for our King to see," the

nobles said to Jean. "Our King will pay you well for your clever cat."

At first the King did not believe the story his nobles told him. He looked at the young stranger, and he stared at the pussycat.

"You say that little creature really kills mice?" the King demanded.

"It does truly, Your Majesty," Jean replied.

"And it can run loose without harm to men?"

"That also is true. If Your Majesty wishes, I will show you just how my cat, Minay, catches mice."

There were plenty of mice in the palace of the King. Mice were playing hide-and-seek under his golden throne. Mice were running over the tables and chairs, and up and down the silk curtains.

Jean set Minay down on the floor. The happy cat jumped first on one little gray mouse, then on another. One by one, she laid the dead mice in a pile at the feet of the wondering King.

"I must have that beast here in my palace," the King cried in delight. "How much gold do you ask for your cat, young man?"

"Oh, I could not sell my cat, Your Majesty," Jean declared firmly. "My cat is the very best cat in the world. She is my only friend. She is my beloved companion."

"I must have the cat," the King said again. "She must kill all these mice which make our days and nights miserable." This King was not used to having people say "No" to him.

"Young man, you shall have half my kingdom in return for your cat. But you must leave her here with me."

"Not for all of your kingdom will I be parted from my dear Minay." Jean stood firm before the King.

"But you need not be parted from the cat, my son," the King smiled. "You, too, shall stay with us. My daughter and I will try to make you happy. We will grant your smallest wish if you and your cat will only live with us here in our palace."

That King and his fair daughter treated their guest with great honor. And, as you may guess, it ended with the miller's son marrying the beautiful princess.

Their wedding was splendid. Everyone cried, "Long live our Princess and the Cat's Master!"

Even more splendid was the feast that was given when Minay, the cat, presented the King with seven small kittens. Everyone cried then, "Long live the Cat and the Little Cats."

So the cat the miller left to his youngest son brought him good fortune. Even as he sat beside the King on the throne, this good young man did not forget his two brothers. He sent them, each one, three bags of gold.

It was just in time, too. For those lazy fellows had never taken good care of the mill, nor of the donkey that turned it. The poor hungry donkey had died. The millstone had stopped turning. The brothers were just about to be put out of their home by the lord of the valley.

With the gold from their kind and forgiving brother, Louis bought another donkey. Paul opened the mill again. The farmers began coming again to have their grain ground.

Let us hope that the two lazy youths had learned a lesson. Let us hope they began to work, and that, after that, all went well for them, too.

Why Dogs and Cats Are Not Friends

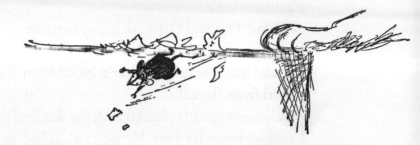

Once upon a time, so the old stories say, dogs and cats lived at peace with one another. They were good friends. They hunted together across the fields. They ate together from the same dish in their master's house. They slept side by side, by the stove in his kitchen.

Of course, even today, that is how it is with some dogs and cats. But everyone knows most strange dogs and strange cats do not like each other. Everyone knows what people mean when they talk about the "dog-and-cat" life of quarrelsome families.

I am not the only one who would like to know why two such splendid animals as dogs and cats cannot be friends. In all times and in all lands, people have tried to find out the reason. Now, in the country called Latvia, they say it happened like this—

When the world was just made, Adam, the first man, had a dog and a cat. Adam had not yet had time to think up special names for his animals, so he called them just "Dog" and just "Cat." No doubt it was God who had told him what they were.

At first Dog and Cat were happy together. They were the best of friends. Where Dog went, Cat went. When Dog ate, Cat ate. There was never a growl from the dog, never a snarl from the cat.

Adam was greatly pleased with the dog and the cat which God had made for him. He never even had to scold them.

Soon there were other dogs and cats in this world. In those times, as now, dogs liked to hunt. It was their nature to kill and eat the small creatures they found in the woods.

All the dogs went out hunting together. And one day they forgot the food they were meant to eat. They killed a fine sheep. It was one of Adam's fattest sheep. And Adam was angry at the dogs.

"I shall complain to God who put you dogs on this earth," Adam cried. And he made all the dogs go along with him to the place where God sat in judgment over the wrongs of the world.

"These dogs have killed a fine sheep," Adam said to God. "They killed one of my fattest sheep, and they ate it up. They should be punished." Oh, Adam was angry, just as farmers today are angry when dogs run after their sheep.

God was angry too. His face was as dark as the storm

clouds he sometimes sends across the sky. And the dogs were afraid.

"We were hungry, O God," the dogs said. Their heads hung down. Their tails were tucked tight between their legs. And they were trying to give some excuse for this wicked thing they had done.

"Hunger comes to all living things," God replied. "It is true one must eat when he is hungry. But I have put food for all here on the earth. The food meant for the dog is the meat of the creatures that are down on the ground."

By those words God meant, of course, the small beasts, like rabbits and squirrels, that run low on the ground. But one of the clever dogs saw that "down on the ground" might be taken two ways.

"Will you write it on paper?" the dog said to Adam. "Will you please write that dogs may eat any animals that are down on the ground?"

Well, when he was home again, Adam wrote on a paper the words God had spoken, that "dogs may eat animals down on the ground."

"Adam's own Dog shall keep this paper safely for us," the other dogs said. "Yes, Dog shall keep our paper for us until it is needed."

So Dog took the paper. At first he never let it out of his sight. He slept with it under his nose. He laid it down beside his bowl when he ate. He even took the precious paper with him out hunting.

It sometimes was hard to know what to do with the paper

when a rabbit ran past him. And one day, when Dog came in from the woods, the paper was wet with rain.

"You had best put your precious paper away some place where it will keep dry," his friend, Cat, said to him.

"Yes, I shall have to put our paper away," Dog agreed. "But where can I put it where it will be dry? Where can I put it where it will not be lost?"

"I know the very place," Cat said to Dog. "Up on top of the master's stove, far back in a dark corner. It is warm and dry up there. Your paper will be out of the way of the broom, too."

You see, in old houses in Latvia, the great stove was built of thick bricks. It had a broad, flat, smooth top. Adam, himself, often slept on top of the stove when the weather was cold.

The top of the brick stove was the favorite napping place of the cat. Cat could easily jump to its warm top from the stool that stood beside it.

"Good! Good! You are wise, Cat." The dog was delighted. "Put my precious paper up there, far back in the corner, well out of sight." Dog could not jump so high himself. He had to let the cat put the paper away for him.

After that, Dog was free to hunt far and wide. Each day he went forth with the other dogs. Most days they found plenty of rabbits and squirrels. But sometimes the rabbits did not come out of their holes. Sometimes the squirrels did not come down out of their trees.

On one such day, the dogs came upon Adam's horse, taking a nap under a tree. Down on the ground was that horse, and sound asleep too.

One of the dogs was more wicked than the others were. At the sight of the horse, he cried, "Here is good meat for the hungry. With so many of us, we could easily kill that horse before he gets up on his feet."

"But Adam will be angry if we kill his horse. God will be angry, too. God said we should take only the creatures that are down on the ground." The other dogs were afraid.

"Is not this horse down on the ground?" the sly dog replied. "Did it not say in our paper that we might eat creatures 'down on the ground'?"

Now those dogs knew well it was not right to eat up a fine horse. Perhaps they were more hungry than usual. Or perhaps they went ahead just for the pleasure of doing something they should not. However it was, they ate up Adam's horse.

Oh, now indeed, Adam was angry. He sent Dog out to bring all the other dogs before him.

"You shall be soundly beaten for this," Adam said to the dogs. "If God does not punish you, I will do it myself. Never shall you have a chance to do such a bad deed again."

"But we have done no wrong," said the bold dog who had led the rest to kill the horse. "You yourself, Adam, wrote it on our paper. 'Dogs may eat animals down on the ground.' Your horse was such an animal. When we came upon him, he was truly down on the ground."

"God did not mean dogs to go around killing horses,

39

any more than he meant they should kill sheep." Adam shook his head.

"Whatever He meant, that is what our paper says," the clever dog answered.

Adam scratched his head thoughtfully. He did not now remember just what the paper did say.

"Show me that paper," said Adam at last. "If the paper truly says that, I will not punish you this time."

"Dog, your own Dog, has the paper in his keeping." All the dogs turned their eyes towards Adam's dog.

"I will go get the paper," Dog cried. And he hurried away to find his friend, Cat.

"Quick, Cat! Come quick! Climb up on the stove and get me our paper." Dog panted as he came galloping into the house.

Quickly the cat jumped up on top of the stove. With his paw, the cat reached far back into the dark corner where he had hidden the paper. But his paw found nothing at all that felt like the paper.

Cat pulled everything out where he could see it. But all he found was a soft paper nest, full of pink baby mice. Oh, it was a fine, soft nest for baby mice. For it was made of tiny, tiny—the very tiniest—bits of white paper. The mother mouse had nibbled them until one hardly could tell what the bits were.

Alas, these bits of paper were all that was left of the precious writing Adam had given the dogs. Who could tell now what words there had been on that precious paper?

Cat timidly told Dog what the mice had done. Dog flew into a rage. He jumped toward the cat. And the cat ran fast as the wind, right out of Adam's house. Dog ran after the cat. And dogs have been chasing cats from that day to this.

Dog himself did not dare to go back to the other dogs. He knew well that they would all jump upon him and tear him to pieces. No one ever saw Dog again. Ever since, all the other dogs have been looking for him.

Surely you have seen what happens whenever two strange dogs meet. They touch noses first. They sniff at each other. That is when the dogs are asking each other, "Are you Dog? Adam's Dog? Do you have our paper?"

Sometimes the strange dogs growl at each other. That is when they are saying, "No, indeed I am not Adam's Dog. Perhaps you are that dog yourself?" Then they call each other names. They may even fight.

Surely, too, you have seen a dog chase a cat up a tree. The dog barks and barks. He is still scolding the cat for not having taken good care of the precious paper.

And when a cat snarls and spits at a dog, he surely is saying, "It was not my fault at all. It was the fault of the mice who chewed your paper to bits."

That is also the way Latvian grandmothers explain why both cats and dogs run after mice.

The Cat
with the Crooked Tail

In other times, in the Far Eastern land of Siam, the king of the country was treated like a god.

"Brother of the Moon!"

"Half-brother of the Sun!"

"Master of One Thousand Elephants!"

"Lord of Four and Twenty Golden Umbrellas!"

These are only a few of the splendid names the people of old Siam gave their King.

No one dared come before the King's throne, except he crawled on the ground. When the Brother of the Moon came out of his shining palace, he rode in a gold chair, carried high on the shoulders of a dozen strong men.

All along the King's way, people knelt down. They bumped their heads on the ground before him. No one dared to lift his eyes to look at this mighty monarch.

In all that ancient kingdom, there was only one who

43

always stood up, straight and proud, before the King. Only one dared to look into the face of the Half Brother of the Sun. And that one was a cat!

Siamese cats of those ancient times were very much like the Siamese cats of today. Their silky coats were pale gold. Their ear tips, their tails, their four paws, and their faces were like shining brown velvet. And their proud eyes were as blue as the very heavens above.

Oh, the Siamese cat was a royal animal. People in Siam knew this well. These pale gold, blue-eyed cats were not for the common folk. Only in the palaces of the King, or perhaps in the house of a prince, were these noble cats to be seen.

"When God made our cat," Siamese grandmothers told the children, "He took the grace of the tiger. He took the sweetness of the lovebird, the beauty of the young deer, and the softness of the dove. He took the quickness of the lightning and the wisdom of the elephant. All these fine things he put together when he made the blue-eyed golden cat.

"But in one way that first cat was not like our cats today," the wise old grandmothers said. "That first cat had no crook at the end of his brown tail."

The old grandmothers knew why this was. Or they said they did. And they told this story to explain how the Siamese cat came to have a crooked tail.

It happened so long ago that no one knows really how long ago it was. But there once was a certain King of Siam. A great king was he. Truly he was a king fit to be called "Half Brother of the Sun." Truly he was Master of One Thousand Elephants.

In this great King's royal stable there were more elephants than you could count in one day. Some were the precious "white" elephants which only kings may ride upon.

These royal beasts were not exactly white. But they had patches of white upon their huge ears. And their small eyes were light instead of dark.

White elephants like these were rare in the Siamese jungles. They were the greatest treasures any king could have.

Yet, even more than his white elephants, did this King prize his favorite Siamese cat. By night the cat slept upon his master's royal bed. And each morning, when the sun rose, it was a soft brown furry paw on his cheek that wakened the King.

By day the cat sat close to his master's side. His silken cushion lay at the foot of the King's golden throne.

You may think it was strange to have a cat in a throne room. Indeed it was odd, especially in such a throne room as that of this King. For it was a bright, shining room. Golden bushes and trees were set along its walls. Their trunks and their branches were only gilded. But their twigs and leaves were pure gold.

The King's throne was gold, too. His pointed gold crown, with its flashing gems, sat high on his head, like a tiny temple. Of gold also was the splendid nine-storied umbrella

45

which was above the King's throne. Gold and rich jewels adorned the King's clothes. His pointed red shoes were embroidered in gold.

The cat, too, wore gold. A fine chain of gold, sparkling with gems, lay around his soft throat. Another gold chain was fastened into this cat's kingly collar. Its end was linked to a ruby ring which the King wore on his thumb.

Even today Siamese cats know how to talk to their masters. Speak to your own Siamese cat, and he will answer. Be silent too long and he will rub his soft body against your foot. Then he will begin to talk, all by himself, in his low, deep cat voice.

Well, it was like that, also, so long ago. Only in those times people could understand the words which their cats spoke.

"No human in all my kingdom is so wise as you, my dear Cat." The King often said these words, as his royal hand stroked the cat's head. Often and often that King asked his cat to tell him what he should do.

Sometimes a hunter would bring a baby white elephant in from the jungle. The hunter would then crawl before the King to receive his reward. Lying flat on the ground before the golden throne, he would hear the King speak to the cat.

"What shall we give this good hunter of elephants, O Wise Cat?"

The man's heart would be glad when he heard the cat say, "Give him ten thousand silver ticals, O King! Give him ten thousand bags of rice, too! A white elephant is without price."

Or it might have been a very bad man who came crawling in.

"How shall we punish this wicked man, O Cat?" the King would ask.

The cat would rub his head with his paw, and he would reply, "Put the iron collar about his neck. Put chains on his legs. Make him a slave!" Oh, that cat had no mercy on people who did not do right.

Now, it happened one day that this Siamese King was taken sick. The royal doctors shook their heads. They could not find out what was the matter with the Lord of the Golden Umbrellas.

"It may be that the Brother of the Moon needs a good rest," they said. "Perhaps your Heavenly Majesty will go in the royal houseboat to your summer palace up the river. The country air may cure your sickness."

The royal houseboat took the King and the cat up the broad Menam River. But there, in the peace and fresh air of the up-country, the King was no better.

"It may be the summer heat is causing the King's sickness. Let the Ruler of the Ocean Tides go down in his glass palace under the lake," the doctors next ordered. With his cat by his side, the King took his seat inside the great box of glass. Its door was closed tight. No water could come in.

Down, down in the cool lake, the glass room was

47

dropped. The King's servants tended him well. The air was somehow kept sweet and fresh. The summer heat did not find its way to the cool bottom of the lake. Fish swam past the glass house. They amused the King well. Yet his sickness did not go away. And he came back to his splendid palace.

The doctors shook their heads harder. "It must be poison!" they said. "Some one is putting poison into the King's drinking cup. It can be nothing else."

They set guards beside the golden goblet from which the King always drank. By day and by night the guards were there. But at some time or other, those guards must have slept. The King grew sicker and sicker.

Then the King's wives took their turn. Each night ten of his youngest wives sat beside the table upon which the golden goblet was placed. But they, too, must have slept. The King grew worse and worse.

"Something must be done quickly," the doctors said, "or our King will die."

"Let me watch over the King's cup," the blue-eyed cat said at last.

"How could you keep awake, Sir Cat?" The doctors shook their heads. They knew how well cats like to nap. They knew how often the King's cat dozed on the silken cushion at his master's feet.

But the King heard the cat's request.

"My wise cat shall guard my cup," the King gave the order.

48

So they lifted the cat up onto the table. There, he lay down close beside the great golden cup.

For a day and a night, for another day and another night, the cat's blue eyes stayed open. Then his eyelids began to close. He knew he could not keep them open very much longer.

"If only I could take just one little nap," the cat said to himself. "I will wind the end of my tail around the foot of the King's goblet. Should the goblet be moved, I shall surely feel it.

The cat's smoky-brown tail curled itself tight around the thin golden base of the King's cup. Day after day, his tail never let go, except when the King wanted to drink.

In all that great palace there was no man so bold that he would dare now to come near the goblet of the King. Well did all know that at the rustle of their clothes, the cat would spring up into the air. Sharp claws would rake any arm near enough to drop poison into the King's cup.

Little by little the King began to feel better. With the poison gone from his goblet, he soon was well again. At last there was no longer any reason to keep watch over his cup.

Everyone cried out, "Long live the Cat! He has saved our Lord and Master."

The King took the pussy up into his lap. He stroked his velvety back. He softly pulled the dark tail.

It was then that the King felt the crook that had come into the tail of his faithful cat. So long had the cat's tail

been curled round the cup, that it could not now unbend.

Never did this little crook disappear from the tail of the King's cat. It appeared in the tails of his kittens. His grand-kittens and his great-grand-kittens had crooked tails, too.

Siamese cats were proud of the little crook in the ends of their tails. They said it proved they were of the same family as this famous cat that saved the life of a king.

From that time on, a Siamese cat with a crooked tail was the most highly prized. It is only in other lands, far, far from Siam, that people do not care whether or not their cats have crooked tails.

The Cat, the Dog, and the Mongoose

"Once again, my children, let all say aloud the first of the Five Shining Rules. Then I will tell you a tale."

It was a yellow-robed Burmese monk speaking to a crowd of small boys who sat about him under the mango tree. The boys were having their last lesson of the day at the temple school. Their small throats were sore with shouting and shouting. Each one had tried to shout the words he was studying louder than the others. Then his teacher would say he had studied the hardest.

It was pleasant in the shade of the mango tree beside the red and gold Burmese temple. A gentle breeze tinkled the bells on the ends of the curved temple roof. The scent of wild flowers came over the great fence of teakwood that ran around the temple yard.

"Thou shalt not take the life of any living thing! That is the first of the Five Shining Rules," all the boys shouted together.

"And now, Holy One, it is time for our story," one of the bolder pupils said softly.

The boys looked up to all the monks in this temple. All through their land of Burma, people honored these yellow-robed priests of Buddha, with their quiet faces and their heads shaved bare. And this Old One, their teacher, was greatly loved by all the boys in the village.

This was the best time of their school day, the boys thought. It was the time for the story with which the Old One always ended his teaching.

"Thou shalt not take the life of even the smallest living thing!" the old monk repeated. "Aye, that is the meaning of the first of the Five Rules. Our great teacher, Buddha, tells us that in the body of an ant, or even a gnat, there may be the soul of someone who once was a man.

"To do harm to any living creature brings bad luck. To do good brings good fortune. That is how it was with the young man, Po See. Listen and learn from his story, my children."

And there, under the mango tree, with his dark eyes shining out of his wrinkled brown face, the old man told the tale. It was this very tale about Po See, his cat, his dog, and his mongoose.

In Burma, long, long ago, there once was this youth whose name was Po See. His father had died, and he lived alone with his mother in a comfortable house. There were servants to wait on them, and they were happy together, this boy and his mother.

Po See had grown to be almost a man when one day his mother said to him, "Soon it will be time for you to take your father's place, Po See. Our house and our lands must be cared for. We have other riches as well. You must learn to look after them.

"Wisdom does not come all at once," his mother said to the young man. "A mountain is climbed one step at a time. You must go out into the world and learn for yourself."

His mother gave Po See money. He had three hundred rupees to pay for what he should need. And she sent three of their servants along with the youth to serve him during the journey.

The young man set forth with shining eyes. This would be an adventure. He would show his good mother how wise and how careful he already was.

They had not gone very far when they met a man carrying a thin, sickly dog. Po See's good heart was touched by the sad eyes of the dog. And he said to the man, "I will buy that dog from you."

"Pay me one hundred rupees for my dog, and he is yours." The man was greedy. That was a big price for such a thin, sickly dog. But Po See handed over the hundred rupees.

"Take the dog home to my mother! Tell her to care for the dog until I come home!" Po See sent one of the three

54

servants back with this message. His mother could not understand why her son had paid so great a price for such a thin, sickly dog. But she did as he asked.

A few days later, Po See met a man carrying a cat. It was a scrawny cat, and it, too, was sick. The youth's good heart was touched.

"Will you sell me the cat?" Po See asked. This man was glad to get rid of the sick animal. But he, too, demanded one hundred rupees.

A second servant brought the sick cat home to the mother of this kind young man. She did not understand why so much trouble should be taken about a sick cat. But she gave it food and a place to sleep in her house.

Another day it was a wild mongoose, whose foot had been caught in a trap. Po See bought it from the man who had caught it. For it he paid his last hundred rupees. And he sent this animal back to his mother by his third servant.

Now the young man was alone. His money was gone. But he was not afraid. He could always find shelter, and perhaps a little rice, too, in the temples along his way.

At Po See's home the cat and the dog soon grew well and strong. The mongoose's foot healed.

It was no trouble at all to care for the two tame animals. But the mongoose was wild. Po See's mother was afraid it would not be happy shut up in her garden. But she put it there under the bushes, and she gave it rice soaked in oil.

But she could see that the mongoose was not content.

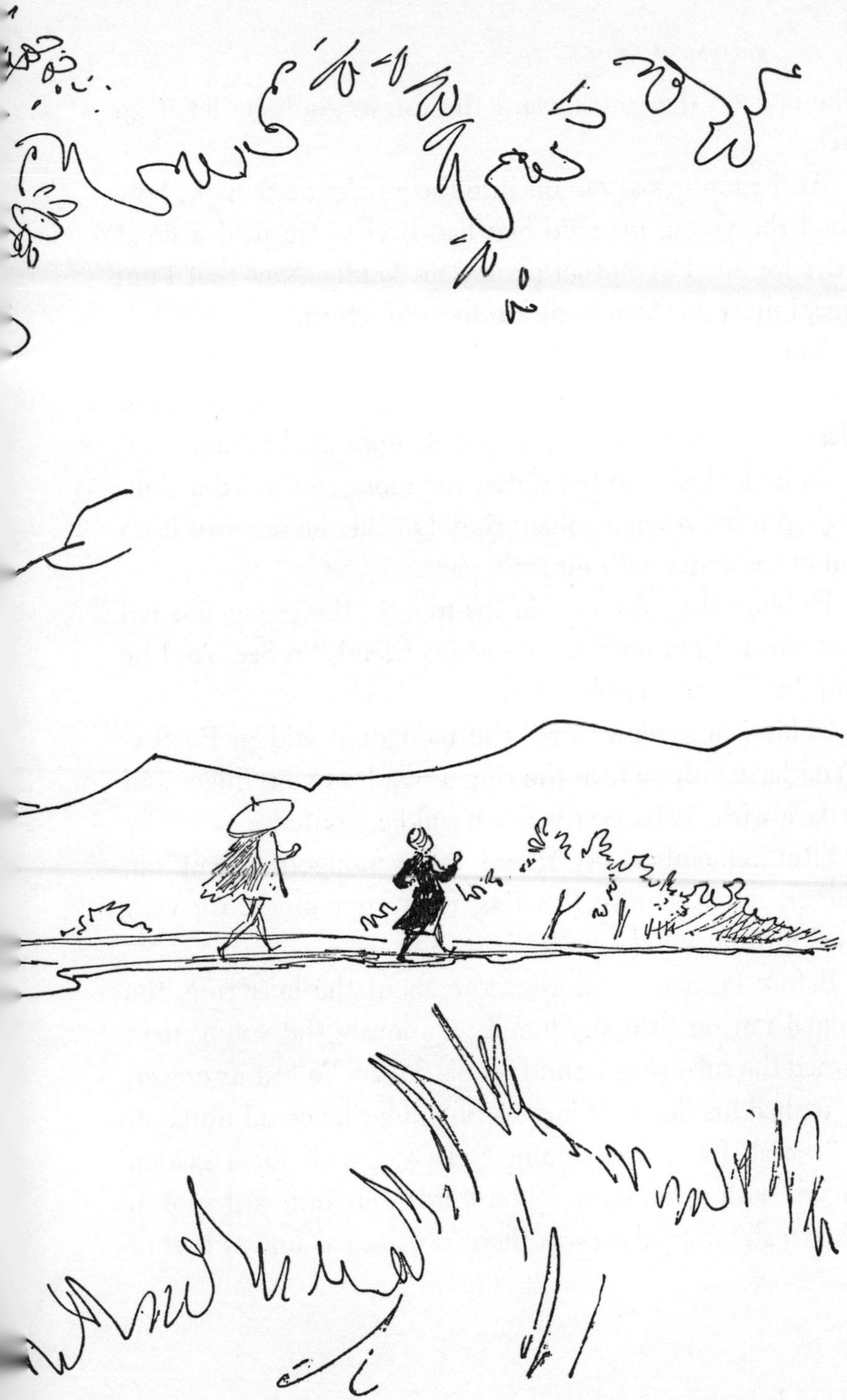

She opened the gate toward the forest. And she let it go free.

As the mongoose ran off into the jungle, he thought how good the young man Po See had been. "He paid a great price for me. His mother treated me kindly. Now that I am free, I must do them some kindness in return."

Soon the mongoose stopped to drink at a forest pool. It was a fairy pool and it belonged to a genie. Its water was so clear he could see every tiny pebble upon its bottom.

As he looked into the water, the mongoose spied a shining red ruby, set in a golden ring. Quickly he scooped it up out of the water with his little paws.

Holding the ruby ring in his mouth, the mongoose ran and ran. He ran until he found his friend, Po See. And he laid the ring down at his feet.

"This is a genie's ring," the mongoose said to Po See. "You have only to turn the ring around on your finger and make a wish. Whatever you ask will be granted."

"But remember, my friend," the mongoose went on, "never, never remove this ring from your finger. Or your good fortune will disappear."

Before Po See could ask more about the fairy ring, the animal ran off into the jungle. Curiously the young man turned the ruby ring around on his finger. To test its power, he wished for the most impossible things he could think of.

"I wish for a fine shining palace. I wish for a golden pagoda with seven roofs." The words were only just spoken when a shining palace was there, a palace as fine as that of

58

the King. A pagoda was there too, covered with gold, and with silver bells hanging from each of its seven roofs.

The King of the land came to see these two wonders. His daughter, the fair Princess Ma Dee, came with him. The King and his daughter were as pleased by the goodness of the young man, Po See, as they were with his shining palace and his golden pagoda.

Such a fine, rich young man surely was just the bridegroom the King would choose for his daughter. And so it happened.

The young couple lived happily in the shining palace. But often Po See had to be away. To pass the time the fair Princess had lessons from a certain young teacher.

The teacher was clad in the robes of a monk. So everyone thought he was a Holy One. No one guessed he was not a monk at all. No one guessed he was wicked and jealous of the good fortune that had come to Po See. The Prince himself did not know that the man in the monk's clothes had found out his ring's secret.

"Why does not your husband let you wear his fine ruby ring?" the false monk said one day to the Princess during her lesson.

"I never have asked him," the Princess replied.

"Oh, perhaps he does not love you as well as his ring?" the sly teacher said.

"That is not true," Ma Dee cried. "Po See loves me better than anything in the world. I know he would let me wear his ring if I should ask him."

59

The words of the wicked teacher troubled Ma Dee. That very night she asked her young husband to let her try on his ring. Po See could not say "No" to his beloved bride. So he put the ring on her finger.

"It is lonely, my dear husband, when you are away from my side. Let me wear your ring while you are gone tomorrow. It will help make the time pass."

"Well, you may wear it, my dear, if you will promise not to show it to anyone, and not to take it off of your finger."

Ma Dee did not guess the secret of the ring. And she wanted to prove to her teacher that her husband loved her dearly.

"See, I have the ruby ring," she said the next day.

"Truly it is beautiful." The sly teacher bent over the ruby. "May I look at this fine stone just a little closer? Perhaps I may hold the ring in my own hand?"

At first Ma Dee refused. But her old nurse, who was with them, cried, "What harm could it do? Show the ring to the Holy One."

No sooner had the false monk put the ring on his finger than he turned it around and cried "I wish I were a crow."

Before the eyes of the startled Princess and her nurse, he turned into a black bird. With the ruby ring in his beak, he flew out of the window.

On, on the thief flew until he came to an island in the midst of the sea. There no one could reach him. He safely could wish himself back into the form of a man. He, too, could wish for a palace and a pagoda.

Po See, at first, scolded his wife for losing his ring. But when he saw how she cried, he wiped her tears away.

"The fault was mine, not yours, my dear," he said to comfort her. "I should never have taken the ring from my own finger. I did not obey the words of my good mongoose."

The cat and the dog soon heard of the bad luck of their friend.

"Po See paid a great price for me," said the cat. "I must help him in his trouble." And he climbed over the garden gate and went to the genie's fairy pool in the forest.

The beautiful daughter of the genie was bathing there. Her clothes and her jewels lay on the bank. The clever cat caught up a shining necklace of scarlet rubies. He ran away with it and hid it under a bush.

"Give me my necklace, Cat," the genie's daughter cried when she came out of the water. "Without my ruby necklace, my fairy power is gone."

"You shall have your necklace," the cat replied, "but only if you will help me get the ruby ring back for my master. Make me a dry path through the sea so that I may go to the island where the robber hides with Po See's ring."

The genie's daughter promised. As soon as she held her magic necklace again, she parted the waters. She made a dry path so that the cat could run over it to find the false monk.

In his island palace, the wicked man lay in a deep sleep.

So deep was his sleep that he did not even feel the cat pull the ring from his hand.

The story of Po See's ruby ring spread through the land. With it again on his finger, the young man grew richer and richer.

One day a band of robbers came to his palace. They planned to kill Po See and to take his magic ring from him.

The robbers were at the very gate of the palace when the dog Po See had saved ran out upon them. Down went their leader! Down went many others under the dog's fierce attack. As soon as they could get onto their feet again, they all ran away.

So the dog, too, repaid Po See for the good turn he had done. The dog saved his master's life, and his ring as well.

As long as they lived, the cat and the dog, and the mongoose too, dwelt with Po See and his Princess. The three animals were good friends at first. But after a time they grew jealous of one another. Each one declared he should be served first when mealtime came.

"I gave Po See his magic ring in the first place," the mongoose said.

"I got the ring back for him when it was lost," boasted the cat.

"I saved his life as well as his ring from the robbers," the dog shouted loudest of all three of them.

Well, the only way to settle the matter was to go to the wise Queen of the land. She listened to their stories—to the cat, the dog, and the mongoose, each in his turn. Then she thought for a long time.

"The mongoose did well when he gave Po See the ring," she said at last. "The cat did well, too, when he brought the ring back to him. But the dog saved his master as well as the ring. It is the dog who should have first place in his master's home."

Then the wise Queen added these words. "No other animals are so important to man as you three. No others know so well how to be faithful. The cat and the dog have important work to do about the house. The mongoose also has his work, keeping snakes out of the garden."

These words of the Queen made the animals happy. They went home together, and ever since then cats, dogs, and mongooses have lived at peace in the houses of men.

The yellow-robed teacher rose from his seat on the ground under the mango tree. The boys got up too. And before they ran off to their homes, the old man said to them, "Remember this tale, my children. Remember that, though he is the wiser, man often is helped by friendship with the animals."

63

Magnificent Hounds of Finn MacCool

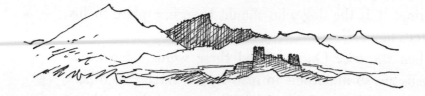

Here's a strange story now. It's about a great hero of early Ireland. And it's about his two magnificent hunting hounds that were known all over that land.

The hero himself was Finn MacCool. "Finn" he was called because of his fair skin and his hair of bright, shining gold. He was a son of the great Cool who, before him, was the chief of all Irish chieftains.

The two hunting hounds were Bran and Skolawn. Finn had three hundred fine dogs, it is said. But the ones he loved best were these two, Bran and Skolawn.

How many dogs went forth with Finn to chase the deer, the old books do not tell us. But it is sure that, always and always, Bran and Skolawn ran by his side.

Why Finn loved these two dogs so well, no one now knows. There are many tales about this shining hero and his magnificent hounds. Many songs that told of their strength and brave deeds were sung about the winter fires of Old Ireland.

One song tells of a wild boar which Finn and his friends met one day in the forest. Other chieftains were hunting along with Finn that day. And their dogs were there, too.

What a great boar that one must have been! The song says it charged the whole company as if it were crazy-mad. Its eyes were like balls of fire. Its mouth dripped with red blood.

In less time than it takes a stone to drop to the ground, the wild boar routed the dogs. Most of the frightened hunters, like their dogs, hid in the bushes and behind the trees.

Only Finn and his two hounds were not afraid of the beast. The dog, Bran, was the hero of that day. Bran flew at the boar. He seized its thick throat. And he shook that great boar this way and that, as if it were only a bundle of rags.

Another song told of the time when Bran and Skolawn saved the life of a little boy. A pack of wild dogs had made a ring around the child. They were snarling and biting each other to get at him.

Finn heard the noise. He heard the deep voices of his two hunting hounds. They were baying and baying, and barking and barking.

"Bran and Skolawn are calling for help. They are in trouble, and they are calling for me," Finn said to himself.

65

And he ran like a deer through the woods to find out what the matter could be.

The sight that Finn saw made his bold heart almost stop beating. A hundred dogs must have been there, to make such a pack. And in their midst were the two forms of Finn's own fighting hounds, Bran and Skolawn.

Jumping and whirling, snarling and biting, the magnificent dogs were holding off the pack. At first Finn could not see what it was they were protecting. With blows of his club to the right and the left, the chieftain made his way through the fighting dogs.

It was then that he caught sight of the little boy whose skin was fair and whose hair was bright as his own. "Gold hair! Fair skin! It is my own little son." Tears ran down the face of the great chieftain as he caught the child up, safe, in his arms.

Well, stories like these might well explain why Finn so loved his hounds Bran and Skolawn. But there was more to it than that.

The secret was that the two hunting hounds were Finn MacCool's own cousins!

You can believe just as much as you like of this old Irish story. It comes from times when people knew more about the Fairy World than we do today. Those were times when men and fairies married each other. Curious things happened, they say, in those long-ago times.

This golden-haired Finn was chief of all chieftains in Ireland then. Men feared him for his fierce anger. But

they loved him for his gentle ways with the weak and the poor.

Now, Tyren was the name of Finn's favorite aunt. She was the dear younger sister of his own mother, but she was not even so old as he was himself. Finn loved her greatly, for she was as fair and as good as any girl in the land.

Fair Tyren had married a handsome hero named Ullan. When Finn gave them his blessing, he said to the hero, "See that you make my dear Tyren happy! May the day never come when she does not go singing through your castle halls! Yet if that day should come, give me your word Ullan, that you will send Tyren back to me safely."

Of course, Ullan gave his word. How could he know that such strange things would happen?

How could he guess that a fairy sweetheart of other days would be so jealous of his young bride? Once he had loved this Fairy Girl. But now it was Tyren he loved as his wife.

How could Ullan foretell that the Fairy Girl would come even into his own castle? But come she did. And there was black anger in her fairy heart.

The Fairy Girl came seeking, not Ullan himself, but his gentle bride. It was with Tyren that she was angry. For it was Tyren who, all unknowing, had taken the Fairy Girl's place in Ullan's heart.

That Fairy Girl was a great one for making magic. Fairy spells to change herself from one shape to another were no secrets to her.

What shape she put on that day, I do not know. But she

68

said she came from the great Finn. So they made her welcome.

It was her magic she used to get even with the fair bride of Ullan. Out in the garden the two young women met. One tap of the hazelwood stick in the Fairy Girl's hand, and straightway poor Tyren was changed into a dog. She became a little hound dog, with soft, gentle brown eyes.

It did not take the Fairy Girl long to put a collar around the neck of this soft-eyed little hound. Quickly she led the enchanted dog away, away from her home. And no one knew where they went.

"Now it is your turn to weep and be sad," the Fairy Girl spoke to Tyren with hate in her voice.

"Your beauty made Ullan forget me, his true sweetheart. Now he shall see that beauty no more. I shall take you far, far from here, where no one will know you are not truly a dog. They shall treat you as you deserve."

But if the Fairy Girl thought men would beat or kick this sweet hound, she was mistaken. One look from the gentle, soft big brown eyes, and their hands fell to stroking the little hound's head.

No one can be sure just what befell poor Tyren in the days when she had the form of a hound. No one knows surely where the Fairy Girl led her. But no harm came to her, at all.

At last Finn heard the news that his beloved Tyren was gone from Ullan's castle. And this is the message the chief of all chieftains then sent to Ullan:

"Remember the promise you gave me when you wed our fair Tyren. They tell me the day has come when she no longer goes singing through your castle halls. Keep the vow you made then. Bring Tyren safe back to me, or you shall feel my anger."

Ullan was as eager to find his lost bride as Finn was to have her back. Ever since she disappeared, her husband had been searching for her.

Ullan and his men looked all through the castle. They looked for her in the forest. They even looked in the river. But no trace of her did they find.

Then someone remembered the strange girl who had come to Ullan's castle that day. Others said they had seen Tyren with the girl out in the garden.

Somehow Ullan found out that this girl was his sweetheart from the Fairy World. Somehow he knew it was she who had taken Tyren away.

"Give me back my dear wife, Tyren!" Ullan demanded as soon as he found his way to the Fairy World.

"What should I know of your wife, Ullan?" The Fairy Girl pretended to be surprised by the question.

"You were the last one to be with her," Ullan insisted.

"Well, what if I do know where Tyren is? Never, never, will I give her back to you! It was me you promised to marry long before she was your wife."

"But Tyren is my true wife. I love her dearly. Besides, Finn wants her back, too." Ullan knew that the fairy folk,

70

also, feared Finn. He hoped fear of Finn might help change this Fairy Girl's mind.

"I will give Tyren back to Finn. I will not give her to you, Ullan. It was indeed I who turned your wife into a dog. It is only I who can give her back her own human form," the Fairy Girl nodded.

"But I will not lift my magic spell from Tyren unless you give me your word that you will make me your wife. Send Tyren to Finn. Take me for your wife in her place. Then, only then, will I set Tyren free." Ullan could see the Fairy Girl meant what she said.

Was it Ullan's love and pity for Tyren? Or was it that he was afraid of the anger of Finn? Whatever the reason was, the hero gave the Fairy Girl his promise to make her his wife.

Together the two of them went to find the enchanted hound. Ullan watched the Fairy Girl touch the dog's head with the magic hazelwood stick. And lo, there before him was Tyren with her own fair face and her own woman's form once again. Tears rolled down the man's face when he thought his dear Tyren would never again be his wife.

That very night there was a knock on the door of the castle of Finn MacCool. Standing there, on the doorstep, the chieftain found his dear aunt, the beloved young sister of his own mother. Not harmed at all, at all, was Tyren, except she was heartsick at losing her husband to the Fairy Girl.

The strangest part of the story is about the basket which

71

Tyren was carrying upon her arm. Inside it Finn saw two puppies, two little hounds with big soft brown eyes.

"Fine little dogeens are these two," Finn said, rubbing their strong backs with his great hand.

"Aye, but these little dogeens are my own children, Finn," Tyren said sadly. "They are the children of Ullan. But they were born to me like this, when I had the form of a hound.

"I begged that Fairy Girl to change my babies into their rightful human shapes," Tyren almost was weeping. "But she said she could not. Puppies they had been born. Puppies they would have to be all their lives long. Oh wirra! Wirra! It breaks my heart just to look at them." The poor mother wiped the tears from her eyes.

"Finn MacCool, you are the best in all this land at caring for dogs," she said. "Will you not take my little dogeens and raise them with love? I give them to you."

So Finn MacCool got his magnificent hunting hounds.

"The best dogs in all Ireland are my hounds, Bran and Skolawn," the chieftain often said. "As brave as the bravest of all the heroes are they. I love these two hounds as if they were my brothers."

That really was not so strange, for after all the dogs were his cousins.

Perhaps you wonder what happened to Tyren after she left the two puppies with Finn MacCool? Well, Tyren was so happy to have her own face and form once more that she soon forgot the wrong she had suffered at the hands of the Fairy Girl.

She was not long without a husband. So fair and so good was she that many heroes wanted to marry her. She chose another chieftain who was quite as handsome and as loving as Ullan had been.

This time, however, before she would marry him, Tyren made sure her bridegroom had never given his promise to any sweetheart from the Fairy World.

The
Hunting Cat

Everyone knows that dogs are good hunters. Many a man prizes his hunting dog almost as much as his best gun. As long as people can remember, dogs have gone hunting with their masters in the deep woods. They sniff out the wild animals from under the bushes. They scare the birds up from their hiding places in the thick grass.

But who ever heard of a hunting cat? Who ever knew a hunter who took a cat with him into the woods instead of a dog?

Well, there was a man like that once. He lived in the northern country of Europe called Latvia. His cat, that man said, was as good as any dog for scaring up birds and for sniffing out beasts.

"I like to take my dear cat along when I go hunting," that man said to his friends. "I talk to my cat. And my cat talks to me. With my cat running beside me, I am not lonely even far, far out in the forest."

Oh, that man was fond of his hunting cat. When they came to a stream of water, even a very small stream, he let the cat jump up onto his shoulder. So the cat did not need to get his paws wet.

Indeed, the cat often rode for a long way up there on his master's shoulder. It was a fine place from which to spy the horns of a deer in among the trees.

One morning the cat saw a big deer with great branching horns. He told his master in time, and the man's gun brought down the deer.

The cat's master was happy. Now there would be meat in plenty for many days in his little house.

The cat was happy, too. For even when they have milk to drink, cats like fresh meat. Straightway this cat began to lick up the blood from the freshly killed animal.

"I never can carry such a big deer home by myself, Cat," the man said to his strange hunting companion. "I shall go get our horse to drag our meat home.

"Guard the deer well, Cat," the man said as he went away. "Don't let any other creature come near it. I will return just as soon as I can."

So the cat stayed behind, close to the deer. He was a good watchman, that cat was. He kept looking around and around to make sure no stranger was near.

But the smell of the fresh deer meat made him feel hungry.

75

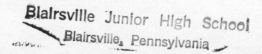

"My master will surely give me my share of this meat," the cat said to himself. "Surely he will not mind if I take a bite or two now, instead of later on." And that is what this cat was doing when some animals, passing by, stuck their heads out of the bushes.

One was a great bear. Another was a fierce wolf. The others were a sly fox and a hare with tall ears.

The bear was first to see the cat there, eating the deer. He could not see very well, for he and his three friends were still quite far away.

"Just look at that, friends," the bear cried. "What kind of fierce beast can this be? He is small, very small. Yet he has killed and is eating up a great deer!"

"From here I cannot tell what kind of beast this one is," the wolf replied. "But clearly it is some terrible animal which we do not know. Take care! Don't go nearer! He might turn upon us."

"We must make him our friend." The hare waved his tall ears in his excitement.

"I know what to do," said the sly fox. "We must make a feast for the fierce little beast. I will run to the farmhouse on the other side of the woods, and get us a goose. Bear will climb up a bee tree and bring down some honey. Wolf will find us a kettle. And Hare will start a good fire to cook the fine feast."

"Yes," all the four agreed. "It is better to make a friend of such a very fierce little animal. Anyone could tell he is fierce. Has he not killed the great deer all by himself?"

76

The hare chose a good place for building the fire. He laid it where the wind would blow the good goose smell from the kettle toward the cat's nose.

The wolf brought the kettle. He set it over the fire with just the right amount of fresh water in it.

The fox pulled all the feathers off of the goose. He licked its skin clean. Then he threw it into the kettle.

The bear dropped in his honey. And all four stood about the pot until the cooking was well begun.

"Now we must hide ourselves. The little beast must not see us until he has eaten the goose," the animals said.

The bear climbed up into a tree. The fox and the hare crawled under some bushes. And the wolf crept beneath a pile of branches and twigs.

"What is that good smell?" the cat said to himself. "Surely it is a goose smell. And surely it comes from near-by."

The cat turned his head away from the deer which he had been left to watch. The goose smell was even better than the deer smell.

Indeed, the cooked goose smelled so good that the cat began to creep toward it. Then he thought how his master had said, "Guard our meat well, Cat!" And he turned back.

The goose cooked and cooked in the pot with the wild honey. It smelled better and better.

At last the cat licked his mouth, and he said, "Oh well, I can still watch our deer from a little distance away. There

77

is no stranger about. It will be quite safe for me to go and find out where this good goose smell is coming from."

Somehow or other, the cat managed to knock the kettle off of the fire. When the goose meat had cooled enough, he began to eat the fine feast which the four animals had made for him.

"Our plan is working," the wolf whispered to the fox and the hare. "When he has had his fill, this fierce little beast will not wish to eat us as he was eating that deer."

In his joy, the wolf's tail beat upon the hard ground. That tail was so long that its end stuck far out of the wolf's hiding place.

Of course, the hunting cat saw only a bit of dark fur moving up and down. He thought, "Here's a young rabbit!" And he pounced upon it.

His sharp cat's claws bit deep, deep into the flesh along the wolf's tail. The wolf was scared almost out of his wits. With a yelp and a howl, he ran off into the woods.

Now for all he was a hunter, this cat was still only a cat. The yelp of the wolf made his fur stand on end. Frightened almost to death, the cat started to climb up the very tree where the big bear was hiding.

"Oh! Oh! I was right," the bear said to himself. "This is indeed a terrible beast. First it killed a great deer. Then it drove the wolf away. Now it is coming for me." That silly bear was so afraid that he fell down out of the high tree, and broke his neck.

Both the bear and the wolf would have done better to go

a little more slowly. Better to find out first what the little beast truly was before they became so afraid.

What do you think happened to the other two, the fox and the hare?

Well, the fox and the hare were both laughing. They were laughing so hard that they could not move. For they had come close enough now to see that their "terrible beast" was only a cat. A little cat had frightened away the big wolf. A little cat had made the great bear fall out of a tree and kill himself.

It is no wonder the two laughed, that fox and that hare. They laughed and they laughed. The fox laughed so hard he split the sides of his mouth almost to his ears. Look well at a fox the next time you meet one. You will see just what happened to that fox's mouth when he laughed so hard at the cat.

The hare laughed too much, too. He laughed so hard that his upper lip split right in the middle. And that is how it is with all hares' lips today.

The fox and the hare ran away when they heard the man coming back with the horse to drag the deer home. And you can picture for yourself that hunter's surprise when he saw his cat sitting beside the dead bear. Always, after that, the story the man liked best to tell was about his cat, the great hunter.

"What a hunter my cat is," he boasted to his friends. "Who of you has a cat, or even a dog, who can kill a great bear all by himself?"

80

The Cat
That Went
to Heaven

In India people once believed that the cat knew the way up to Heaven. The gods love the cat, they said, above all other beasts.

"The man who harms a cat will surely be punished," they told their children. "For every tiny fine hair in the cat's furry coat, that man will have to carry a tree out of the forest. He will have to pile the trees up, one on the other. A cat has so many hairs that the poor man's pile of trees will reach high into the sky."

Then sometimes they told the children this story about two holy men, a king, and a cat that once went to Heaven.

One of the holy men was a priest of the Indian god Brahma. The priest was a wise Brahman, and a great teacher, too. Many people sat at his feet to listen while he read from the holy books.

81

The other man in this tale did not know much about books. But he, too, followed the ways of the gods. He was a Yogi, which is to say he thought only about Heaven.

The Yogi could do the most impossible things, so this story tells us. He could walk barefoot across a bed of red-hot coals. He could sleep on a bed of sharp-pointed nails. He was sure these hard tasks pleased the gods.

Then, as now, there were many holy men like these two in India. But of all the holy men, then, these two were the most holy. The Brahman and the Yogi agreed upon that. Somehow, however, they could not agree upon which of them was the holier.

The Brahman said, "Surely it is I who please Heaven the most, for I teach many others the way of the gods."

The Yogi said, "Nay, it is I whom the gods love. I think of the gods all day and all night."

Each time they met, the Brahman and the Yogi argued like this. They argued so much that, at last, they asked the King to decide which of them was the holier.

"All the day long, I sit without food, O Fountain of Wisdom," the Braham told the King. "I sit on the hard ground under a banyan tree. From the holy books I teach the Way of the Gods to those who crowd around me."

"All the day long, and all the night, too, I lie on a bed of nails," the Yogi said. "So hard do I pray that I do not feel the sharp points of the nails. Crowds come to watch me when I walk barefoot over the fiery coals. I show them what man can do when he thinks of the gods."

"I cannot choose between two such holy men," the wise King declared. "Both of you are good men. Both surely are greatly loved by the gods. The gods must decide between you."

"I will go up to Heaven and ask the gods, myself." Tho proud Brahman was bold enough to make this boast.

"No man can enter the home of the gods," the Yogi declared. "The gods will not let you come into even the very lowest of their seven heavens."

"The Yogi is right," the people in the King's court whispered to one another. In the seven heavenly kingdoms there lived only the gods and the goddesses, so they believed. Millions of gods there might be in the heavens, but not one single man.

"Surely it will be different with me," the proud Brahman boasted. "The gods will not turn away a holy man such as I. To prove my welcome in Heaven, I will bring back a flower from the gods' Life-Giving Tree." Oh, he was indeed a bold man, that proud Brahman.

The Yogi was happy when he saw the Brahman start out on his heavenly journey. He did not think his rival could ever make good his boast. Surely the gods would not part with even one magic flower from their Tree of Long Life.

The King was happy, too. If he could but sniff the sweet smell of the Heavenly Flower, he knew he would live forever and ever.

But the happiness of the Yogi lasted only a short time. The very next day the Brahman came back in triumph. In

83

his hand he held the magic blossom from the Heavenly Tree. He said that the gods themselves had given it to him.

"This one is the holiest. The honor is to the Brahman," the King declared.

"All honor to the Brahman who was welcomed in Heaven!" the men about the King shouted.

But the Yogi raised his voice, crying, "Wait! Wait! Your Greatness is too easily satisfied. If this Brahman could enter Heaven, then anyone can. Even my cat! Yes, I will send my cat up to Heaven. My cat also shall bring back a flower from the Tree of Long Life." That Yogi was even bolder, you see, than the proud Brahman.

The Yogi did not feel quite so bold when he went to his home to get his cat. He took the little animal up into his arms. And he repeated the foolish words he had spoken to the King.

Now, the Yogi's cat was a fine cat, as fine a cat as there was in all that broad land. And as wise a cat, too!

"Do not worry, my master," the cat purred to comfort the Yogi. "It may well be that I can find the way up to Heaven. The gods love all living things. Perhaps they will indeed let me come in."

Everyone was dumb with wonder when they saw the Yogi's cat leap from a tall treetop up and up into the clouds. They waited and waited to see the cat fall down to the ground. But no such thing happened. Their necks grew tired with stretching. Their eyes ached as they looked and looked into the sky.

84

But the cat did not appear. One day, then another day! Another and another! Still the Yogi's cat did not come back.

"We cannot wait much longer," the King said to the Yogi at last.

"Have patience, O King! Have patience a little while longer!" the holy man begged. And he sent up prayers to the gods that his cat might return.

In Heaven the gods had welcomed the cat, as the Yogi had boasted. The cat had no trouble at all in coming before the very throne of the Great Brahma.

The gods gave the cat a thousand pats on his soft back. And the one who petted him most was a beautiful wife of the Great Brahma, himself. She was the goddess whom men call Saras Vati.

Saras Vati gave the cat heavenly cream to drink. And all the gods listened to the cat's story about his holy master, the Yogi.

"You shall have a great branch, all covered with blossoms, from the Heavenly Tree," Brahma said to the cat when his story was told. "And you shall take it back to your good master, the Yogi."

But the goddess Saras Vati loved the Yogi's cat so much that she did not want him to go back to the earth. She held the cat on her lap, and she stroked his soft fur. It was because of her that the Yogi's cat did not come back right away.

How many days, or months, or even years, it was, the tale

85

does not say. But the King and his people did not grow any older, for the gods made time stand still.

At last, one day, the cat said to Saras Vati, "My good master, the Yogi, must be in great trouble. Let me go back to him now! Let me take him the branch from the Tree of Long Life!"

Saras Vati still wanted to keep the cat by her side. But the Great Brahma took pity upon the poor Yogi.

One morning there was a strange light in the sky above the Yogi's bed of nails. People ran out of their houses to see what it could be. They brought the King out of his palace. And all looked up at the sky.

Across it there floated clouds bright as jewels. Topaz clouds, emerald clouds, and clouds the color of rubies and amethysts! In the midst of these rainbow clouds, the wondering people saw a golden throne. And sitting upon the throne was the cat of the Yogi.

Shouts rose from the crowd about the King. For beside the cat on the throne there was a great flowery branch from the Heavenly Tree. Not just one blossom but many were there for all to smell.

"The honor goes to the Yogi. His cat has brought many more blossoms to earth than the Brahman." This was the cry that rose on all sides.

Now it was the turn of that proud Brahman to call out, "Wait! Wait! O King!"

"It was not this Yogi who brought these flowers from

86

Heaven," the Brahman said. "It was his cat. It is the cat, not the Yogi, whom the gods love."

"The Brahman speaks truly," the wise King said slowly. "But still the cat belongs to the Yogi. It was for the Yogi that the cat went up to Heaven. It was to the Yogi that the gods sent down the great branch from their Tree of Long Life. Surely they love the Yogi too."

The King thought and thought. He could not, even yet, choose between the two holy men.

"Only one thing is sure," the King declared. "The cat of the Yogi is the most splendid cat in my kingdom. I will give him a thousand rupees for his cat. The cat shall live in my palace. He shall sleep on my soft couch. He shall eat at my royal table."

After that, when the King sat on his throne, the cat often slept at his feet, or even upon his lap. From far and from near people came just to have a look at this famous cat. Many wanted to ask the cat the way up to Heaven. The story does not tell us what the cat replied.

Don't Beat
Your Dog

Samba's village was deep, deep in the heart of Africa. Its grass huts stood on the banks of the river Nile. It was far up that great river, far from the sea, almost at the place where the river begins. And the people who lived in that village belonged to a tribe known as the Denkas.

There were many dogs in that Denka village on the river Nile. One of them lived in the shadow of Samba's own house of grass. Mostly the boy was kind to his dog. He played with the dog. He gave the dog heads of the fish he caught in the river. He gave him bones from the meat animals his father brought in from the forest. Truly this Samba was fond of his dog.

But one day Samba was cross. He was cross with everybody and everything. What had gone wrong that day, I do not know. But there was no smile on Samba's brown face. And before the day ended he even was beating his dog with a stick.

The poor dog howled. He howled so loud that Samba's

grandmother looked up from her seat on the ground by the door of their grass hut.

"Samba! Samba!" she cried. "Don't beat our dog!"

But the angry boy went on laying his stick against the sides of the poor beast.

"Samba! Samba!" the African grandmother cried again. "Don't beat our dog. Have you forgotten? It was the dog who first gave us our fire to cook our food with! We owe our dog thanks for our fire, instead of blows."

The boy dropped his stick. He came close to the old woman. And he squatted down on the ground close to her feet.

"How did the dog give us fire, Grandmother?" Samba asked curiously.

The old woman smiled. A story always made her grandson forget he was cross. And she told him this tale while the dog licked his sore sides.

It wasn't so long ago that there was no fire at all on this earth. Luckily the Denkas did not need a fire to keep themselves warm. All the year round the sun was hot in their sky. Where they lived the trouble was to keep themselves cool.

But the Denkas would have liked to have fire for cooking their food. They needed to cook the porridge they made from the grain that grew on the banks of their river. They needed to cook the meat the hunters brought home from the forest.

When a man caught a fish in the river, he cut it up into pieces. He put it into a pot and set it out in the sun. The heat from the sun melted the fat on the fish. Then that man could drink the warm, melted fish grease. He could eat the pieces of fish that had slowly cooked in the sun.

Cooking with the sun's heat was also the only way the Denkas had for making their meat ready for eating. And cooking that way took a long time. Children often cried from the hunger that came with such long waiting.

"If we only had fire!" the Denkas said to each other.

Once, long ago, there had been fire in their land. But that fire had gone out. They knew of no way, now, to get more fire for their cooking.

Well, there was one Denka who had a dog in his hut. And that dog used to go hunting, all by himself, far out in the forest.

One day the dog went farther away from home than ever before. Before he could get back, a storm swept over the land. Such a big storm it was! Rain fell like a hundred waterfalls out of the sky. So hard did the water come down that it beat the leaves off the trees.

The poor dog looked this way and that way to find shelter. He was glad when he came to a hole in the ground big enough for him to crawl into, out of the storm.

This big hole turned out to be the home of a huge snake. It was the home of a giant boa. Luckily the giant boa was a friendly snake. It made the dog welcome.

"Come in, friend, come in!" the boa said to his visitor. "Come dry yourself by my fire!"

Sure enough! There was a fire burning there on the ground in that boa's home.

This dog did not know much about fire. This was the very first fire he ever had seen. He could feel his coat drying out in its bright warmth. And he crept toward its flames to see just what it was.

Closer, closer he went, until the boa cried out, "Take care, my friend! Don't go too near! That fire will burn you."

"Thank you, thank you, for the warning," the dog said to the snake. But his eyes were fixed on the fire, and he kept crawling closer. At last, when he turned around to lie down, his tail swung into the flame. And its hair caught on fire.

"Ow! Wow! Ow! Wow!" the dog howled.

He ran out of the snake's hole as fast as ever he could. He ran and he ran, but he could not get rid of the pain of his burning tail.

The storm now was over. The hot sun was shining again, down on the land. Just as the boa's fire had dried the wet coat of the dog, so the hot sun had dried off the wet grass and bushes.

In his pain, the dog with the burning tail rolled in the long grass. This was a wise thing for him to do. For it quickly put out the fire on his tail. But, of course, it also set fire to the grass he was rolling in. And the fire spread.

From one leaf to another! From bush to bush, the flames went. Oh, that was the biggest fire anyone can remember.

92

The Denkas saw its red light as it swept through the woods.

"Fire! Here is fire! Fire for our cooking, if we can catch it!" they shouted to each other. And they ran with their pots to bring the precious fire back to their huts.

The Denkas made a fine feast for that dog. They put grease on his burned tail. They gave him a place on their sleeping mats. And ever since then no one, except perhaps some very cross boy, has ever wanted to beat their good friend, the dog, who brought them their fire.

Ever since that day, too, people in Africa have taken care not to let their cooking fires go out. Who knows, another time their dogs might not find a boa's hole with a fire in it?

The Bad Boy
and the Good Dog

Here is another story about a boy who treated his dog badly. This one, also, was an African boy who lived by a river.

I don't know the dog's name, but he was a good hunter. Everyone in the village said he was truly a good dog.

Koko was the boy's name. And everyone in that village said he was a bad boy. That was because he liked to tease and play tricks.

If a pot was upset on a neighbor's cooking fire, they said, "Koko has been here."

If his father's hunting spear was missing, the man always called first, "Koko! Koko, where have you hidden my hunting spear?"

If the smaller children built playhouses of grass down by the river, they always kept watch lest Koko come near. They

95

knew he would knock their playhouses down with his feet.
Often he would try to frighten the littlest ones by saying, "The lions are coming. You had better run into your
huts."

The dogs of that village knew better than to get in the
way of this bad boy. He pulled their ears until it hurt. He
twisted their tails. He even beat them with long sticks.

One day, when he had nothing better to do, Koko was
walking on the bank of the river. And his own dog was beside him.

That good dog loved Koko. Even the boy's teasing did
not make the dog bite him.

There were many log boats there on the banks of the
river. And first Koko thought he would go out in one, all
by himself. It did not matter to this bad boy whose log boat
he should take.

Koko had picked out a very good boat. He was about to
push it off the riverbank into the water, when his eyes fell
on his dog. And a wicked, cruel thought came into his
mind.

"Come here, Dog," he called. "You shall go out on the
river instead of me. It will be a funny sight to see a dog in
a boat all by himself. The river will whirl you around and
around. It will carry you down to the rapid waters. It will
dash your boat on the rocks. Then we shall see whether
you can swim to shore." The cruel boy laughed at the
thought of how frightened the poor dog would be.

Now this African dog was not afraid of the water. He

knew how to swim. But he did not like the river because of the great crocodiles that lived in it. Their huge jaws and their sharp teeth could quickly make an end of a dog, or of a boy.

Also, the dog had never before been in a log canoe. He hung back when Koko tried to make him jump into the boat.

The bad boy grabbed his dog by the neck. He swung him into the boat. Then he gave it a great push. This sent the boat out into the swift river. The rushing water turned it around and around. Oh, the dog was frightened then.

Koko was frightened even more badly. For when he gave the boat the great push, he lost his footing on the riverbank. The boy fell into the swift water. And he fell so hard that his breath was almost knocked out of him.

The swift river rolled Koko over and over. It carried him far out into the stream. It brought him almost to the log canoe where the dog crouched low in his fear.

Koko was not near enough to catch hold of the boat. He swam and he swam, but he never could reach it. He tried and he tried. But somehow he could not swim close enough. Always he kept looking around for fear of a crocodile.

In the log boat the good dog stood up and barked. He barked and he barked. If anyone on shore heard the barking, no doubt he said, "Oh, that is Koko's dog. Koko is teasing his dog again." And no one came to pull the boy out of the river.

97

Koko was growing tired with swimming and swimming. At last he went down, down, down under the water. He brought himself up again. But again he went under. Truly the boy was just about to drown.

Then it was that the good dog jumped into the river. He swam to the boy and caught hold of his jacket. It was lucky that jacket was made of strong cotton cloth. It was lucky, too, that it was well fastened about Koko's body. For the jacket did not tear apart. It did not come off.

The dog dragged the boy close to the log boat. Somehow or other Koko was able to climb into it, and his life was saved.

People in that village would have been surprised to see Koko lift his dog gently into the log canoe. Koko was surprised himself. He did not feel like teasing his dog any more. He was far too thankful that his life had been saved.

How did the two of them get back to the village? Well, it would have served Koko right if the river had carried his boat down to the rapids, and thrown it on the rocks. But the good dog began to bark again. Koko shouted for help. And this time the man whose boat the boy had taken was the one who heard the noise.

Quickly the man jumped into the river. He pushed a paddle before him as he swam out to the boat. And he brought Koko and his dog safely back to the riverbank.

That was a fine lesson for this bad boy. The story says that Koko stopped all his teasing. The tricks he played no

longer made other people unhappy. In the village they no longer called Koko the "bad boy."

Mothers and grandmothers there told this story again and again. The children all listened. They liked this tale about the bad boy and the good dog who saved his life.

Bobo, Black Dog, and the Cannibal Woman

From Africa also—from Basutoland—comes another curious story. In this one there are a boy, a black dog, and a cannibal woman.

It really is true that not so long ago there still were people called cannibals in that land. They ate other people. They thought no more of eating a man than of eating an elephant or a monkey. Some say that the cannibals liked man's meat far better than animal meat.

The story begins with a poor man and his wife who had too many children. Try as they would, they never could find enough food for them all.

"We shall have to go away from this place," the man said

to his wife one day. "We shall have to go to some other place where there is more food."

So they set out. The man and the woman and all their children walked over the land. Each one carried his bundle upon the top of his head. They made a long line when they walked, one behind the other.

At one place they came to a very deep river. There was no bridge across it. And the river was too deep for them to walk through its waters.

So the father found a log big enough for one person to ride upon. He pushed the log ahead of him as he swam to the other side of the stream. First his wife rode over the river on the log. Then, one by one, he pushed the children across.

Over and back! Over and back! He pushed them all over, all but the very youngest child, Bobo. This boy, Bobo, was small. He was sickly and weak.

Perhaps his father did not care a great deal for Bobo. Or perhaps he was tired with pushing that log over the river. At any rate he decided to leave Bobo behind.

"Bobo is too weak and too sickly to stand the trip to our new home," the cruel man said to his wife. "We have quite enough children without him. I will leave Bobo behind. I will leave Black Dog to look out for him."

Bobo's mother wept. Because he was so small and so weak, she loved him the best. But she could not change her husband's mind.

"Good-by, my dear Bobo," she called over the river.

"May no harm come to you! Keep Black Dog close beside you! Black Dog knows well how to look out for himself. He will look out for you, too."

All alone with Black Dog, Bobo could not help crying. But he soon was so hungry that he forgot to cry. It was all he could do to find something to eat.

Bobo was a clever boy, for all he was not very big. On the ground at his feet, he saw a long line of ants. Each ant was carrying a little grain in his mouth. Each one marched behind another as they all hurried along the forest path.

"Come, Black Dog," Bobo cried. "Let us see where those ants are going with the good grain."

The boy and the dog followed at the end of the procession of ants. And soon they found themselves at the mouth of a clean, dry, big cave. Just inside the cave's mouth, there was a great heap of the good grain where the ants had piled it up.

"Here is food for us, Black Dog, good food!" Bobo said. Somehow the boy managed to pound that grain into meal. He mixed the meal with water, and he cooked it in cakes. There was enough grain in that cave for himself and Black Dog, and for the ants too.

But after a time the boy began to be lonely.

"We cannot stay here always," Bobo said to his dog. "Let us go find some village where there are people. Perhaps some kind family will give us a place on their sleeping mats."

As they went through the jungle, Bobo remembered the

103

words of his mother, "Keep Black Dog beside you. Black Dog knows well how to look out for himself. He will look out for you too."

So the boy watched everything his dog did. And he did the same. They came to a stream, and Bobo was thirsty. Black Dog also was thirsty. His long red tongue hung far out of his panting mouth.

But the dog did not drink out of that stream. So Bobo did not drink either. And that was good. For the boy soon saw in the water an animal that was dead. Surely such bad water would have made both the dog and the boy sick.

The next stream was clear and cool. Black Dog took a long drink. Bobo drank, too. And they went on, feeling better.

The boy and the dog went on and on through the forest. For ten days and more they walked. And then they came to a village where there were huts in plenty.

The curious thing about this village was that there were no men or boys in it. The only people Bobo met there were women and girls.

"You must not stay here, boy," the women said to Bobo. "It is not safe for any man or any boy in this village. Old Dimo, the Cannibal Woman, lives here. She does not eat women or girls, but no man or boy can escape her."

"I am too tired to go farther," Bobo replied. "Black Dog will look out for me. My mother said so. I am not afraid."

To show that he truly was not afraid, the boy made his way straight to the hut of the Cannibal Woman.

104

"Good day to you, boy," Old Dimo, the Cannibal Woman, spoke to him kindly. "You look tired and hungry. You need rest and food. Come into my hut and I will give you a fine dinner."

"I will come in, Grandmother, but Black Dog must come with me." Bobo was a brave boy, even though he was weak and small.

So Bobo and Black Dog went inside the hut of Old Dimo. She set down before them dishes of porridge and meat. Secretly, she had put sleep medicine into the meat. When Bobo was deep in sleep, she meant to eat him.

Bobo waited to see what Black Dog would do. When the dog ate the porridge and left the meat in the dish, the boy did the same.

"Why do you not eat your meat, boy?" Old Dimo asked.

"It is the custom in my home village to eat only the porridge," Bobo replied.

At the next meal, the Cannibal Woman put the sleep medicine in the porridge and not in the meat. Again Bobo watched to see what his dog would do.

The dog ate up the meat and left the porridge alone. Bobo did the same.

"Why do you not eat your porridge, boy?" the Cannibal Woman asked crossly.

"Oh, in our village often we eat the meat and leave the porridge alone." Bobo was ready with his answer.

When night came, Black Dog lay down close beside

Bobo on the sleeping mat. Old Dimo thought they both were asleep. She came creeping quietly, quietly, across her hut to them.

In her old brown hand she was holding a very sharp knife. She raised it above Bobo. But before she could hurt the boy, Black Dog bit her arm. Her knife fell to the ground, and she did not dare to try anything like that again.

In the morning the boy and his dog went out of the hut of the Cannibal Woman. All in that village were surprised to see them still alive. They shook their heads, and they cried out, "Take care, boy, take care! No good will come to you from Old Dimo."

While Bobo and Black Dog were gone, the Cannibal Woman dug a deep pit, just at her door. She covered the big hole in the ground with branches and leaves so Bobo should not see it.

But when they came home that night, Bobo saw that Black Dog did not go in by the door. He jumped into the window. So the boy jumped in after him. And Old Dimo's plan to have Bobo fall into the pit did not succeed.

"Why did you not come in by the door, boy?" Old Dimo cried.

"Oh, back home in our village, we often come into our house by the window. It is our custom." Bobo replied carelessly, as if it were no great matter.

Next day the Cannibal Woman dug a trap, too, under the window. When Bobo and Black Dog came back at dinnertime, the dog started toward the window as before. Then he turned away and sat down on the ground. Bobo turned away too. He, too, sat down on the ground.

"Why don't you come in, boy?" the Cannibal Woman asked angrily.

"Oh, I don't want any dinner," Bobo said easily. "I'll just stay outside."

"Then you shall help me gather firewood in the forest," Old Dimo declared. "And you shall leave that black dog behind. He would only be in the way."

At first Bobo said no, he wanted Black Dog to go with him. Then he either forgot what his mother had said. Or he let the Cannibal Woman talk him into leaving Black Dog behind.

Out in the forest, Old Dimo sent the boy up into a tree. She gave him a sharp ax. And she told him to chop off a branch.

As Bobo began to cut the tree branch, the Cannibal Woman gave a horrid laugh.

"Now I have you where I want you," she cried. "You thought you were smart not to eat the food I fixed for you. You thought you were clever not to come into my house by the door or the window. But I have you now. You shall not get away."

"I will never come down out of this tree," Bobo said boldly.

"Oh, yes you will. If you will not climb down, I will cut the tree down."

"But I have the ax." Bobo was beginning to be afraid.

"And I have my strong teeth," the Cannibal Woman screamed as she danced around the trunk of the tree. "I shall bite this tree in two."

Old Dimo set her great teeth into the trunk of that tree. She bit into it as easily as you would bite into bread. Then Bobo began to be truly afraid.

"Black Dog! Black Dog!" he called with all his might.

"Black Dog! Black Dog! Here! Here! Come save me!"

Black Dog heard the boy's cries. He came bounding into the forest. And he bit the old woman until she let go of the tree.

The dog held the Cannibal Woman down on the ground. His teeth held on tight to her woolly black hair. As Bobo began to climb down out of the tree, his ax slipped from his fingers. Its sharp edge fell just on the neck of the Cannibal Woman. And it cut off her head.

There was joy in that village when Bobo's story was told. The men and the boys came out of their hiding places in the deep woods. The wives and the mothers wept for gladness to have their husbands and their sons back in their homes.

Young though he was, they made the boy, Bobo, chief of that village. Whenever there was an elephant hunt, they let Bobo throw the first spear. When the meat was cut up, Bobo had the first bite of roast elephant foot. Black Dog always had a juicy elephant bone to chew upon.

No one ever told me whether it happened, but I cannot

help hoping that Bobo's father someday came to that village. I should like to have seen his face when he saw once more the boy he had left on the riverbank. I should have liked to see that man bow down before the young village chief who was really his son.

The Holy Cat
of Tibet

Have you ever heard of the country in Asia which men call Tibet?

Tibet is a land of very high mountains. Up, up, its mountains rise into the sky. They shut that bleak, chilly country away from its neighbor lands.

Tibet is a land, too, of yellow-robed lamas with closely shaved heads. These lamas are the priests of the wise teacher, Buddha.

Not so very long ago the lamas ruled in Tibet. They lived in splendid palaces. They built many temples in which they said their prayers to Buddha. The lamas then were the richest of all those who lived in that land.

So it is not strange that there should be a lama in this

111

old story which comes from Tibet. It is not strange either
that the cat in this tale chose a lama to copy. It happened
like this——

Once there was a cat that lived in Tibet. He was a big yellow cat, with fur the same mustard color as the robe of a
lama.

Now, this yellow cat was a rascal. He stole food from the
kitchens of the lamas. Indeed, that cat got his living by
stealing food. He stole the milk which the lamas got from
their yak cows. He ate up the lamas' yak butter, as well. And
he stole other things besides food from the priests of the
wise Buddha.

One night the yellow cat even stole a lama's prayer
beads. And this was worse than stealing yak milk or yak butter. No lama could say his prayers to Buddha without his
string of beads. How should he know how many prayers he
said without counting a bead for each one?

When that lama caught the cat making off with his beads,
he was angry. He ran after the cat. That lama's legs fairly
flew under his long yellow robe.

The cat's legs flew faster, however. And the cat reached
the gate first. Just as the animal squeezed himself under the
gate, the lama grabbed him by the tail.

With all his might, the cat tried to get free. At last he
succeeded. But one might say it was only by a hair's breadth.
For that lama held on so tight to the cat's tail that most of
its hair was pulled off.

112

The cat ran away as fast as he could. He ran far up into the mountains where the lama never could find him. And he hid himself in a cave there until the hair grew again on his bare tail.

Well, that was all right. The cat was safe. And his tail soon was covered with hair as before. But there was no food in that cave. Not even one mouse came along. Soon all the bugs and the beetles were eaten up, and the worms too. The cat knew then he would have to go back to the town.

The yellow cat walked along the highroad, thinking what he should do now. He knew he would not dare to go back to steal from the lamas as he had before.

All he had brought with him was the string of prayer beads that belonged to the holy man. The beads swung from his neck as he went along. They tapped him on his forepaws, and he looked down at them.

"Prayer beads bring good luck to the lamas," the cat thought. "Why should not these prayer beads bring good luck to me? Who has more to eat in this land than the fat, yellow-robed ones? It is a fine thing to be a lama. I have a yellow coat and a lama's prayer beads. I will become a lama myself."

Not far out of the town, the yellow cat sat himself down by the side of the road. Like a true lama, he kept touching the beads on the string round his neck. He was sitting as still as any lama when a fat field mouse poked his head out of the grass on the edge of the road.

At sight of the cat, the mouse turned to run. But the cat

113

called to him, saying "Do not be afraid. I am a Holy One. Behold my lama's prayer beads. With them I say my prayers to Buddha, a prayer for every bead. As Buddha teaches, I hurt no living thing. Nothing that flies! Nothing that creeps! My old ways are put aside. I have joined the Holy Ones of the Yellow Robes."

"Wonder of wonders!" the mouse cried aloud. "I must go tell the others."

At first the other mice would not believe such a miracle could take place.

"He had true lama's prayer beads around his neck," the field mouse declared. "He said he was a lama. He declared he would hurt no living thing, just as Buddha teaches."

The other mice had to see this wonder for themselves. They could not believe there was a cat in the world who would not kill a bird or a mouse.

Oh, the cat lama was clever. He played his part well. The mice always found him purring his prayers out loud. As he prayed, his paw touched a bead for every prayer.

"Will you stay and hear my prayers?" the cat asked the mice. "I will teach you the Way of Life. But you must keep very quiet. And when I have finished, you must make a procession in honor of Buddha. One behind the other, you must walk past me. You must look neither to left nor to right. And you must not look behind either, until you are again in your homes."

There was a reason for this strange order, as you shall see. Each day the long line of mice marched past the cat lama. All looked straight ahead until they were again in their holes.

All reached their holes safely except the very last mouse in the line. Somehow or other that unlucky one never got back to his hole.

Since they did not look behind them, none of the mice saw what the false Holy Cat did. In truth, every day he pounced on the last mouse of all. And he ate it up.

The mice knew that many of their brothers and their cousins were missing. There were now fewer and fewer mice running over that part of Tibet. The matter was talked about. But no one could tell how it came to be so.

"The cat is at the bottom of it," the mice began to say to each other. "Surely he is the one who is killing us off. For all he wears prayer beads, that cat is no lama."

"What do you eat now, O Lama Cat?" the mice asked one day.

"I eat grass, roots, and berries. They are not very good, but they keep me alive," the sly cat replied.

On their way home that day—and not far from the cat either—those mice found a pile of mouse bones. They found some bits of soft gray fur and a lot of mouse whiskers. They were sure then that the cat was telling them lies. There was no truth at all in the cat's saying he would harm no living thing.

Still they could not find out how the trick was done. Even when all were gathered to talk of it, they were not sure.

"We need a bell for the cat," the oldest and wisest mouse

115

said. "It should be a small bell. It should be a shining brass bell such as the lamas take with them when they beg from house to house."

"What shall we do with the bell?" one of the youngest mice asked.

"We shall hang the bell around the neck of the cat lama. If the cat really sits quiet all the day long, then the bell will not ring. But if we hear the bell, we shall know our cat is up to his old tricks."

That very night, two bold mice crept into the house of a rich lama. Together they brought away from it a small shining bell. It was just such a bell as the lamas ring when they go through the land begging. Only it was much smaller.

The mice laid the shining bell down at the feet of the yellow cat.

"We bring you a present, Cat Lama," the oldest mouse said. "It is a lama's bell. You shall use it when you go begging. Then you will have better food in your begging bowl. You will not have to starve upon grass, berries, and roots.

"You shall wear our bell round your neck. It will be another sign that you are truly a Holy Cat."

The cat could not think up any excuse for saying "No." Besides, he liked the golden shine of the little bell. He sat very still while two of the mice fastened the bell round his neck. He thought it would look pretty under his chin.

Next day, when the time for morning prayers came, all

the mice were there. They listened, quite still, to the cat purring his prayers.

At last all the prayers were said. All the beads had been touched. As before, the mice marched, one by one, in front of the cat, and without looking back.

The very last mouse was just passing the cat when the bell rang. At its first tinkle, the mice all looked around. There was the cat, gobbling up his mouse for that day.

Squeaking and squealing, the army of angry mice fell upon the cat. Rats ran to help them. Together they drove that wicked yellow cat from his place by the road. Never again did that sly creature dare to say he was holy.

In the battle between the cat and the mice, the lama's prayer beads fell from around the cat's neck. Perhaps the holy man who owned them found his beads there in the dust when he came home that day with his begging bowl.

The small shining bell, however, was tied on too tight. How the cat got it off, the tale does not say. And while it still hung on the cat's neck, the mice always knew when he was near.

The Dog
That Fought
a Duel

In the great hall of a certain old, old French castle, there is a huge fireplace. Its beautiful chimney piece is made of gray stone. Upon it there are flowers and birds, and animals too.

The most curious carving on this chimney piece is in the very center. It is where all can look upon it and wonder.

There, neatly cut into the gray stone, is the likeness of a dog. It is a splendid dog, a great English bull. And that bulldog is fighting with a knight of the olden times.

Why should a dog fight with a man? Well, this is the way they explained it there in that castle.

119

It is a story about a noble knight and a wicked knight, and a brave dog that loved his good master truly. It happened in times when there were many brave knights and fair ladies in the land of France. Sometimes two knights fell in love with the same lady. Then there was sure to be trouble.

That is how it was with the noble knight, Sir Roland, and the wicked knight, Sir Garin. Both loved a fair lady whose name was Amelie. But the Lady Amelie loved only the good, gentle Sir Roland.

Sir Garin was a bold knight, but a knight with an evil and jealous heart. He ground his teeth in rage when he saw that Roland carried the bright kerchief of Amelie in the tourneys. Jealousy ate at his wicked heart. And he vowed to destroy his rival for the love of fair Amelie.

One day Sir Roland was riding alone in the deep woods. No other rider was near him. No companion did he have with him, except his faithful bulldog. Cesar, this dog was called, like the famed Roman emperor of long, long ago. The name fitted him well. Truly he was a noble dog, truly a royal beast.

Like his master, Cesar was gentle as a friend, yet fierce in the chase. Swift and strong the dog was, true, and always at his master's side at home or abroad.

It was while the dog, Cesar, was chasing a hare that the jealous knight, Garin, rode softly up behind Roland. Before the good Roland could turn to see who was there, Garin threw his lance. Its sharp point pierced Roland's back. It found his great heart, and he fell from his horse dead.

"We will bury the knight's body here, under this tree," Sir Garin said to the servant who came riding after him. "No one need ever know how Sir Roland came by his death. With him out of the world, my way will be clear to win the love of my fair lady."

But Garin forgot the dead knight's faithful dog. When he and his servant had ridden away, Cesar lay down upon his master's grave. There, out in the forest, by day and by night, the dog was on guard.

At Sir Roland's manor house, his servants wondered. The knight's horse came home alone. There was no one riding upon him. They did not wonder greatly that Cesar was not there. They knew the dog would be wherever his master was.

Days went by. Yet Sir Roland did not return. His servants went looking for him. But the forest was big. There were many paths which their master might have taken. None rode into the lonely path where Cesar was standing guard.

The dog found no food during his watch. At last he was so hungry that he was forced to go in search of something to eat.

The first house Cesar came to was that of a friend of his dead master. In that house, often and often, the dog had been fed with the hounds of its owner.

"Cesar, Sir Roland's dog, has come into our courtyard. And he is alone," the servants told the knight of the manor.

"We have fed the dog well, yet he does not wag his tail.

Again, yet again, he howls. It is as though someone were beating him."

The knight, the good friend of the dead Roland, came out to see the dog for himself.

"Truly it is Cesar. How thin and sick he looks! And where is his master? Never have I heard a dog cry in such misery."

"Something is surely amiss with Sir Roland," the knight of the manor said. "Look, the dog runs to the open gate of the courtyard. Now he runs back again. He whines like a child."

"The dog bids us go with him," the knight said to his guests, who had joined him in the court of the manor house. "Let us mount and follow him."

The knights rode after the dog, who kept well ahead of them. Straight as an arrow, Cesar led them to the tree under which the wicked Sir Garin had buried his master.

With all his might, the good dog started digging under that tree. It was no time at all before the knights, digging with him, had uncovered their dead friend and carried him home.

Not long after, the dog, Cesar, met up with Sir Garin. Sir Garin was on foot, and at once the dog leaped upon him. The other knights in the company, all joined together, could scarcely pull the dog off.

The same thing took place again, and yet again. Each time the dog met the man who had killed his dear master, he jumped for his throat.

122

"This is strange," the knights said to one another. "Cesar is gentle with all of us. Only with Garin is he so fierce. It is as if the dog goes mad each time Garin is near."

"Cesar is a dog that loved his master truly," one of the knights said. "Can it be that Garin had something to do with the good Roland's death?"

"Garin hated Roland with all his heart," another knight remembered. And all in that company shook their heads, wondering.

The talk grew and grew. It spread over the land until at last it came to the ears of King Louis VIII. Sir Roland had been greatly beloved by the King. And the strange tales of the knight's dog roused his royal curiosity.

"Let the dog, Cesar, be brought here!" King Louis gave the order. "Let the knight, Garin, come before me at the same time. I would see this strange feud with my own eyes."

At the King's court the noble dog, so gentle with others, growled at Sir Garin as if he would tear him to pieces. When they let go his leash, the dog sprang at the knight. The King's men had to make haste to save the man's life.

"What means the anger of this noble dog?" the King demanded of Garin.

"How should I know, Sire?" the knight replied. "It is true there was no liking between the dog's master and me. Perhaps that is the reason."

"How came the good Roland to his death, Garin?" the King asked of the knight then.

"How should I know that either, Your Majesty?" the wicked knight put on a false look of surprise. And indeed there was no proof that Garin had a hand in the killing of Roland.

In those days, when proof of bad deeds was lacking, the matter often was settled by two men fighting each other. A "duel" was the name for such a battle.

It was believed then that a duel always brought out the truth. God always gave the victory to the one who had the right on his side, or so people said then.

"It is plain that this dog accuses this knight of his master's death," the King said that day. "We have no witnesses. There is no proof. Let the truth be shown by a duel between the man and the dog."

"A duel between a man and a dog! What a strange kind of a duel that one would be!" The nobles in the King's court were struck dumb with surprise.

"A duel, a fair fight, it shall be," King Louis said again. "God will show us the truth. God will not let such a wicked deed go unpunished. The man shall fight the dog fairly. God shall decide."

The place was chosen. The time was set. The weapons were decided upon. The dog was to fight with his sharp teeth, as nature intended. The man was to arm himself with a club.

A big empty barrel was laid down upon its side. Into this the dog might go to get his breath now and then.

It was a strange duel indeed, that battle between the man

and the dog. The signal was given. The dog was set free. The knight swung his club while the animal charged at him fiercely.

Now a blow landed upon the dog's body. Now the animal took a bite out of the man's leg.

Most of the time the whirling dog kept well out of the way of the man's flying club. When he was tired, Cesar ran into the barrel. There the knight's club could not get to him. Sir Garin dared not bend down to look into the barrel, lest the dog snap off his nose.

The duel went on and on. Secretly most of the onlookers hoped that the brave dog would win. No one had much love for the wicked knight, Garin. And all admired this bold dog who loved his master so truly.

At last the knight moved more slowly. His strength was giving out. The blows of his club now were feeble. But the dog was as fresh as when the duel began.

At last, with a mighty leap, the dog knocked Sir Garin down. He grabbed the knight by the leg. The King's guard ran to save him. But they could not pull the dog off.

"Confess! Confess!" rose the cry on all sides.

"God has shown us the truth," the King cried. "Say how the deed was done, Garin. And it may be the dog will let go."

The terrified knight then told the story. And then, so they say in that French castle, the dog let go his hold on the man's leg.

What the punishment was for this wicked knight, I do

126

not know. And what happened to Cesar, I only can guess. Surely, surely, some one of Sir Roland's friends—perhaps even the King himself—took the brave dog into his castle. Who would not gladly give shelter to a dog who could love a master so truly?

Shippei Taro
and the
Monster Cat

There are mountains in Japan, many, many mountains. Little paths wind their way along the steep sides. They run this way and that, so that a traveler may come over the mountains.

Here and there temples have been built by the wayside. And in these live good priests who make travelers welcome.

When the sun shines on the mountainsides, the traveler is safe. His path is clear. He can see the temples from afar.

But when the storms come, fog hides the paths and covers the temples. It is easy, so easy, to lose one's way then.

128

That is what happened to a young Japanese soldier long, long ago. This soldier was a "samurai," a brave young warrior of those ancient times. His name was Yamato, and his sword often was drawn to protect the old or the helpless.

It was a thick fog that caused this Yamato to lose his way there in the mountains. Night was upon him. The rain beat on his back. He was glad, indeed, when a tumbled-down temple showed up out of the mist.

"A poor place is this," the young samurai said to himself. "The steps are falling down. The walls are beginning to crumble. It is no wonder that the priests of this temple have gone away. Yet under its roof, I can sleep dry, out of the rain."

Yamato wrapped his warm cloak about him. And he lay down in a corner of the great temple hall.

It was just before midnight when Yamato suddenly woke out of his deep sleep. Strange noises were ringing through the lonely temple.

"Those sounds are like the yowling of one hundred cats," the young man thought.

And that is just what they were. Rising from his hard bed on the temple floor, Yamato could see all the cats in the light of the moon. The storm was over. The fog had blown away. A silvery moon had come from behind the breaking clouds.

A full hundred cats were dancing about in the great hall of the temple. A hundred cat voices, there, were raised in strange songs. It was truly an eerie sight. Truly these sounds made the samurai's hair stand up on end.

Now and again, Yamato thought he could hear one great cat voice that was louder than all the rest. Once he was sure the voice sang this song:

"Sh! Sh!
Not so loud, pray!
Or Shippei Taro
Will come our way."

For a time, then, the cat voices were lower. But their dancing grew wilder. Soon, once again, that lonely temple hall rang with their yowling. And Yamato heard the great cat voice a second time:

"Beware! Beware!
Have a care! Oh,
Your noise will surely
Wake Shippei Taro.

"Sh! Shippei Taro!

"Sh! Shippei Taro!"

"Shippei Taro! Shippei Taro! Who and what can he be, this Shippei Taro?" Yamato asked himself. It seemed that the dancing cats truly feared someone, or something, named Shippei Taro.

At midnight the dancing cats disappeared. The temple was quiet again. But Yamato did not sleep. There was something about this lonely temple that made him afraid.

Yamato was glad when, at last, the sun found its way in

through the temple door. As soon as it was day, he hurried away, down the mountain.

At its foot, in the valley, there was a small town. And Yamato stopped at the very first house he saw. The young man was hungry. He hoped he would find kind people there who would share their breakfast with him.

In that house there was a man and his wife and his pretty daughter. The three welcomed the young samurai. They brought him a bowl of steaming hot rice and some bean sauce to go with it.

"My thanks are yours, my good hosts," Yamato said when he had eaten. "I feel much better now. But as I ate your good rice, I could not help seeing that all three of you have been weeping. Is there trouble in this house? How can I help you?"

"Alas, Honorable Samurai, we are truly in trouble." The man wiped his eyes. "But there is no help for us. All this valley is cursed by the Monster Cat of the Mountain. High up on the mountainside, in an old temple, lives this evil spirit who takes our daughters from us.

"Each year, on a certain day, each village must send a fair maid to dwell with the Monster Cat. Many have gone. But none has ever returned to her home. If we do not send our daughters to the Monster Cat, every man, woman, and child in this valley will be killed. Tomorrow, alas, it is our beloved daughter, O Koyo, who goes to wait on the Cat."

"Can no one kill the Monster Cat of the Mountain?" Yamato asked his host, wondering.

131

"Our bravest young men have tried," was the reply. "But all have failed. No man in this village now would dare to stay long in the Monster Cat's temple. They all run down the mountain as soon as they have set down the maid they take up from the valley."

Yamato was thinking and thinking about what he had heard, himself, in the old temple.

"Tell me, my good host," he asked his new friend, "do you know anyone by the name of Shippei Taro?"

"Indeed, yes. Shippei Taro is the dog of the Prince of this very valley. Everyone knows the brave dog, Shippei Taro."

The good people wondered at their guest's question. They wondered still more when he told them what he had heard in his night on the mountain. And they dried their eyes when he said he had a plan to save their dear daughter.

"Lend me your brave dog, Shippei Taro, this night, Honorable Sir," Yamato said to the Prince of the valley. "With Shippei Taro to help me, I will try to deliver your people from the curse of the Monster Cat of the Mountain."

The samurai first led Shippei Taro to the house of O Koyo. The girl was weeping again. At her gate stood the open wood box in which she would be carried up to the Monster Cat.

"Do not cry so, O Koyo!" the young man comforted the pretty maid. "Not you, but Shippei Taro is to ride in this box tonight."

It was no trouble to get the young men of the village to help with the wood box. Led by Yamato, they took it up the steep mountain path.

But none wanted to stay there with Yamato, once the box had been set down in front of the temple. Small stones on the path rolled down in showers under their running feet as they hurried away.

Yamato hid himself behind the big wooden box. Then he waited for the Monster Cat to appear.

Just before the hour of midnight, there were the sounds of many cat feet. Out of the temple, the cats came, pell-mell. Cats, cats, and more cats! And at their head was the Monster Cat. He was a great tomcat, fully as big as the big dog, Shippei Taro.

"Wurro-ow-ow-ow!" At the sight of the box, the Monster Cat sent his cry ringing over the hills.

"Wurrow-ow-ow! Wurrow-ow-ow!" Yowls rose from all the cat throats. And they began their horrid dancing about the wood box.

Just then Yamato, the brave samurai, tipped over the box. And the great dog, Shippei Taro, leaped out upon the cats.

"Shippei Taro! Shippei Taro! Beware, it's Shippei Taro!" the cat voices cried. And they all ran back into the temple.

The Monster Cat, who was nearest, did not have time to get away. The brave dog pounced upon him. It was a terrible fight. The tomcat scratched and bit. He clawed and he spit. But the great dog fought even more fiercely.

133

Shippei Taro held the cat down on the ground while Yamato's sharp sword finished the battle. Soon the Monster Cat lay there, dead, at the samurai's feet.

Then the strangest of all these strange things took place. The hundred cats inside the temple were gone. In their places were a hundred fair Japanese maids.

They were the daughters of the valley folk, who had been bewitched by the Monster Cat. Each time a young girl was set down before the temple, the Cat put his spell upon her. Now that the Monster Cat had been killed, his spell no longer had magic.

You can picture for yourself the joy in that valley when Yamato and Shippei Taro led the girls down to their homes.

"Honor to Yamato! Honor to the brave samurai!" the shouts came from all sides. Everyone wanted to lay rich gifts at the feet of this brave young man.

"It was mostly Shippei Taro," the modest Yamato declared. "Honor should first go to brave Shippei Taro."

"Honor to Shippei Taro! Shippei Taro! Shippei Taro!" they all cried then. And every day, after that, a bowl of food was set out before each house in that village for the brave dog.

The Old Man
and His Dog

Every Japanese boy or girl knows this story. Some call it the
Tale of the Old Man Who Made the Dead Trees Blossom.

I like to call it the Tale of the Old Man and His Dog.
For without his dog, the Old Man would not have been
able to make the dead trees come alive again. Without his
good dog, there would have been no story at all.

The Old Man and his Old Wife loved their dog dearly.
There were no children in their house. Their dog was their
only pet. Each day they gave their dog food that was as
good as their own. They gave him thick pieces of fish, not
just the heads or the tails.

In return, that dog loved the two kind old people. He
followed them about at their work all the day long. He
watched their house well at night. Oh, he was a good dog,
just as they were good masters.

The only one who was not good in this story was the man
136

who lived next door. They called him "The Neighbor," but he was by no means a good neighbor. He was a cross, cruel fellow who did not mind kicking a dog out of his way. And the Old Man's dog was afraid of him.

One day the Old Man and the Old Wife were at work in their bean patch. Their dog was sniffing and sniffing along the ground not far away.

All at once the dog stood still. He began to bark. And with his strong toenails, he began to dig up the earth. The dirt flew into the air like a small fountain.

"Look at our dog! What is he doing?" the Old Wife called to her husband.

"I'll just go and see," the Old Man said. With his own digging tool in his hand, he walked over to the hole the dog had made in the ground.

"Come here, Wife! Come! Come, look at this!" the Old Man held up a piece of gold money.

Wonder of wonders! The dog had uncovered a pot filled with gold coins. It was a rich treasure his dog had found for that Old Man. With the gold, he was able to buy food for himself and his wife. He had some, as well, to give to the poor who came to beg at his door.

Everyone marveled at the Old Man's good fortune. The countryside rang with the praises of his wonderful dog.

One day the Neighbor knocked at the Old Man's gate.

"Lend me your dog, Old Man! Let your dog dig in my garden. Let him uncover a treasure, also, for us," the Neighbor said.

"But there may not be gold in your garden," the Old Man replied to the Neighbor. "Besides, you do not like our dog. You kick him and beat him. Often you have warned me to keep him off your land."

"It is different now," the jealous Neighbor replied. "We will treat your dog well. I will not kick him, and I will feed him fresh fish. And why should there not be gold on our land as well as on yours?"

The Old Man could not think of a good answer to this. So he took his dog over to his neighbor's garden.

But the dog remembered too well the times the Neighbor had kicked him. He tried to run home. He would not eat the fresh fish. And he would not dig at all.

The Neighbor had to drag the dog along by a rope. He led the animal into all parts of his garden, crying "Dig, Dog, dig! Why don't you dig?"

But the dog would not dig.

At last, however, the dog stopped at the foot of a bush. He sniffed the ground there, and the Neighbor called out to his wife,

"Ha, here is our treasure! Surely the dog smells something here."

The Neighbor brought his own digging tool. He dug and he dug. But all he uncovered was the bad-smelling body of a dead cat.

Oh, that man was angry then! So angry was he that he struck the dog with his digging tool. He beat him and beat him until the poor dog was dead.

138

"Where is my dog, Neighbor?" The Old Man came looking for his pet that night.

"I killed him. I killed your dog because he did not find any treasure for me. All he found was the bad-smelling body of a dead cat."

Tears came into the eyes of the Old Man.

"And what have you done with my dead dog?" the sad Old Man cried.

"I buried your dog under your own pine tree, there by the road." This was the unfeeling answer of the cruel Neighbor.

That night the Old Man and his Old Wife could not eat their supper for weeping. They put the dog's bowl, filled with fish, on his grave. This was in case his hungry spirit might still be there.

That very night, too, the Old Man had a dream. He thought his dear dog came and spoke to him thus:

"Make a grinding bowl for your rice out of the wood of the pine tree under which I am buried. It will serve you well, Master, as I always served you."

Next morning the Old Man cut down the pine tree. And he made a big bowl for grinding his rice.

"Now, Wife, bring the rice," the Old Man cried, when the bowl was smooth and ready.

Only a few grains of rice were poured into it. But, before the eyes of the old couple, the wood bowl was suddenly full. Rice grains flowed out over its edge. A great river of rice ran out of the bowl that was made from the pine tree by the dog's grave.

The money the rice sold for made the Old Man rich once again. And it made his Neighbor even more jealous than he had been before.

"Lend me your magic grinding bowl, Old Man," the Neighbor begged. "I have rice to grind. And my bowl is small." He hoped that the magic rice bowl would bring him riches, too.

But when the Neighbor poured in his rice, it turned black and sour. It was not fit to eat. And no more rice came out of the wood bowl.

The Neighbor was so angry that he smashed the wood bowl to bits. He set those bits on fire, and he burned them to ashes.

That night the dog again walked through the dreams of the Old Man.

"Gather up the ashes of the rice bowl," the dog said in that dream. "Think of me as you use them, and they will work magic for you. You have but to sprinkle a few ashes on the dead cherry tree out in your garden, and it will come back to life."

The Old Man went to his Neighbor and asked for his rice bowl.

"Oh, I broke it and burned it." That low fellow did not even say he was sorry.

"Ai-ya, my fine bowl!" the Old Man was sad. "Well, at least give me the ashes from its burning."

141

He gathered the ashes up in a box. Then he took them to his cherry tree. He threw a few of the ashes upon its dead branches. At once tiny buds came out upon the brown twigs. Before the wondering eyes of the Old Man and his Old Wife, blossoms like a pink cloud covered the dead tree.

All in that land heard of this Old Man who made a dead tree to blossom. From one town to another, he went with his box of wood ashes. Rich presents were given him when he worked his magic.

News of these strange happenings came at last to the ears of the Prince of that part of Japan.

"Let this Old Man come to our own gardens," the Prince said. "We would see him work his magic upon our royal trees."

There in the Prince's garden, the Old Man brought fresh blossoms out upon a dead cherry tree, a dead peach tree, and a dried-up plum tree.

"Let the Old Man be given ten rolls of fine silk!" The delighted Prince heaped gifts upon this maker of magic. "And let him hereafter be called 'The Old Man Who Makes the Dead Trees to Blossom.'"

From that day, the old couple wore kimonos of silk. The fame of the Old Man spread into every corner of Japan. And, of course, this was more than his jealous Neighbor could bear.

"Those ashes were from the pine tree which the Old Man cut down. Why should I not burn more of its wood and make magic ashes for myself? I have watched the Old Man. Like him, I shall just sprinkle pine ashes upon the dead trees. Then the Prince will reward me, as he did the Old Man."

With a box of pine ashes upon his back, the Neighbor went to the Prince.

"I, too, can make dead trees come alive," he boasted to the men at the palace gate.

"Let him try his magic, too!" the Prince said when they told him of the Neighbor's boasting. And the Prince stood near to watch.

The Neighbor threw a handful of ashes on the dry branch of a cherry tree. But not one single bud came through its brown bark. Not one tiny leaf appeared. There was only dry wood.

A breeze blew over the tree, and the ashes flew into the eyes of the watching Prince. Ashes blew up his nose and into his mouth. The Prince's eyes smarted with pain. He coughed and he sneezed.

"Oh! Ah-choo! Ah-choo! Take this man away and punish him well for telling lies!" The Prince was angry indeed.

Bruised with his beating, the Neighbor crept to his home. In the goodness of their kind hearts, the Old Man and his Old Wife felt sorry for him.

"Good deeds bring good luck," the Old Man said. And he carried a bowl of rice to the house of his jealous neighbor, who had treated him so badly.

What good luck next came to the Old Man, I do not know. But he had the pleasure of doing a neighbor a good turn. It may be that the Neighbor had learned a lesson. It may be that he changed from a bad neighbor into a good one. That is what should have happened.

The Cat and
the Prophet

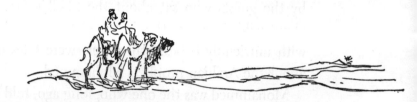

One evening there were guests in a black goat-hair tent on the Arabian Desert. Two friendly riders had come galloping there, over the sandy plain, just at the sunset.

"Riders! Oh, riders!" Adi and his sister, Hamda, had shouted the news to all the black goat-hair tents. As was the custom in the desert, the children's father, the Sheik, had come out himself to make the strange riders welcome.

After the evening meal, the men leaned comfortably back against their camel saddles. These had been put down on the sandy tent floor. They were arranged in a circle about the fire hole.

Adi, being a boy, was allowed to come into the men's side of the black tent. He handed the tiny brass coffee cups around after the men had finished eating. Then, without being noticed, he squatted down behind his father's camel saddle.

Hamda, being a girl, had to stay in the women's part of

145

the tent. But there was a slit in the black goat-hair curtain that divided this Arab home into its two parts. Through this slit, Hamda, too, could see and hear what went on at the coffee circle.

These Arabian children loved to listen to the stories told by the guests who sat about the Sheik's fire. Some were about wild rides over the desert. Others were about battles with unfriendly tribes. Still others were tales of magic, or about the Arabian prophet, Mohammed.

Mohammed was the one who, long ago, told these desert people about God, whom he called Allah. The Arabs believed that Allah gave Mohammed the power to work miracles, or magic.

Both Hamda and her brother, Adi, believed in magic. Each child wore a magic charm to keep bad spirits, or jinn, away.

When Hamda had a toothache, she said it was because a jinni had flown into her mouth. The ache did not go away until her mother hung a special toothache charm round her neck.

This charm was a bit of paper wrapped up in goatskin. Its magic came from the words of Mohammed which were written upon it. These words, Hamda said, drove the jinni out of her tooth.

When he had whooping cough, Adi wore another charm. His charm was in a little goatskin case. It, too, had the words of Mohammed, and Adi said it kept the jinn from tickling his throat.

146

Since they believed in magic charms, it was not strange that these Arab children believed tales of magic. This is one of such tales which they heard told at their father's coffee circle. Adi, from his place behind the camel saddle, and Hamda, on the other side of the goat-hair tent curtain, believed it really happened.

"May Allah give you long life! Allah is great! And Mohammed is his prophet!"

This was the way that story, and all stories like it, began.

The tale is about Allah. It is about Mohammed, the prophet who told men about Allah, and about Mohammed's friend, a cat. It tells why a cat has a long life, and why a cat always lands on his feet.

Once, long ago, the Prophet Mohammed, was spending some time in a town on the edge of the dry Arabian Desert. It was a town built under tall date palms about springs of cool water.

You would think that the Prophet would have stayed there under those palm trees, out of the hot sun. But, instead, he walked far, far out into the desert, where no trees would grow. The only growing things there were a few gray, dry bushes, and there were not many of these.

No doubt Mohammed wanted to be alone under the great sky when he talked to Allah. For he walked far out from the town before he laid his prayer rug down on the sand.

The Prophet knelt down on the small bright-colored rug.

147

He bent his forehead to the ground again and again as he said his prayers to Allah.

Mohammed was a mighty prophet. The Arabs say so. And it was true. He was no doubt truly beloved of Allah.

But for all he was so great, Mohammed was still only a man. The sun was hot on his head, as it is on your head and mine on a sunny hot day. The stones on the sandy desert floor hurt his feet, just as they would hurt our own. Like many desert travelers, Mohammed was tired with his walking over the rough ground.

So when his prayers were said, Mohammed lay down on his bright-colored rug. In the shadow of a desert bush, he fell sound asleep.

While the Prophet was sleeping, a snake crawled out from under that bush. There can be no doubt but that this snake had been sent by Allah's enemy, the Evil One. For there was poison in the snake's bite.

Without making a sound, the snake glided over the sand to the side of the sleeping Prophet. Its tiny forked tongue darted in and out, in and out of its open jaws. Its sharp fangs were ready.

Why does the snake not like men? And why do men not like snakes? Who knows the answers to questions like these?

Some think that snakes were on the earth before men. Adi and Hamda heard that tale, too, one night in their goat-hair tent. Men came later, the storyteller said. They came riding on horses and camels into the desert, where the snakes already were living.

The snakes thought nothing of this at first. The men and their horses and camels were strange. But the snakes did not fear them in the beginning.

Then many, many more people came. The feet of the men's horses and camels crushed the creatures that crawled on the ground. The King of the Snakes sent out spies to see what could be done to drive men out of their desert land.

"Men have clubs to strike us with," the spies told the Snake King. "They throw stones down upon us. Their horses and their camels can run faster than we can crawl. We snakes never could win a war with these men. Never could we drive them out of our land."

"We shall have to hide from these men. We shall have to keep out of their way under the bushes and rocks," the Snake King said to his people. "We shall make holes in the ground where men cannot find us. Allah has given snakes deadly fangs. Our fangs will protect us."

So, on this day in the desert, that snake was ready to use his fangs on the sleeping Prophet. What the Evil One had told him, we do not know. Whether the Prophet's horse had stepped on a snake sometime or other, we do not know that either.

The snake drew back his head. He was ready to strike. But just at that moment, something sharp bit into the snake's tail.

The snake hissed. He looked back to see what was hurting him so.

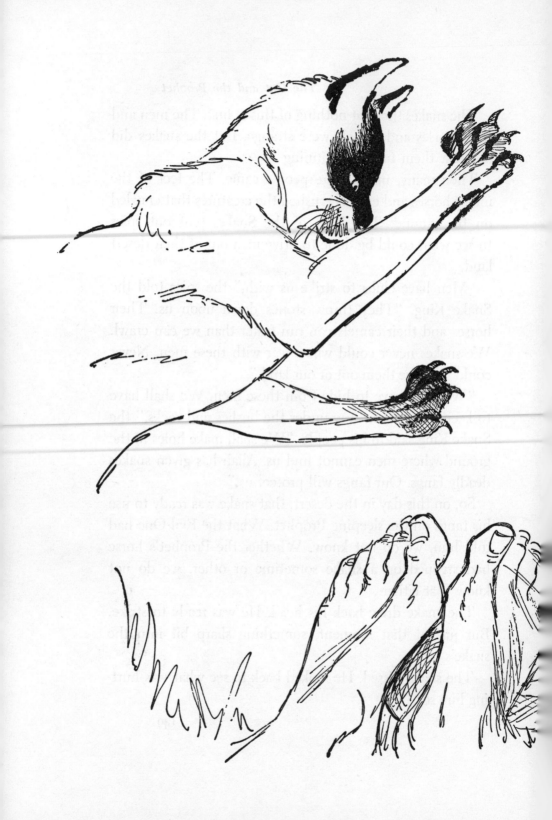

It was a cat! Now, I cannot tell you how a cat came to be so far out in the desert. Perhaps it had chased a mouse over the sand, all the way from the town. Or perhaps it had followed at the heels of the Prophet.

It was an angry cat. A cat whose hair stood on end all along its back! A cat whose eyes flashed like fire! And a cat whose sharp teeth had a firm hold on the snake's tail!

The snake quickly forgot all about the sleeping Prophet. He shook his long body to try to shake the cat off.

The snake twisted and twirled. He tried to bite the cat with his fangs.

The snake lashed his tail and the cat from one side to the other, then up and down. But still the cat held on.

Again and again, the snake tried to bite the cat. But somehow or other, the cat was always out of his reach.

Again, and another time, the cat lost his hold upon the snake's tail. But before the snake could wriggle away under the bush, the cat's teeth took hold of another part of his body.

I should like to have been there—at a distance, of course. I should like to have seen that exciting battle between the angry cat and the spotted snake.

The noise the two made, fighting there on the sand, woke up the Prophet. Mohammed raised himself up on his elbow to see what was going on. He was just in time to watch the cat finish the battle. Soon the snake lay still, dead on the desert sand.

"Well done, O Cat!" the Prophet cried out. "May thy

cat tribe be blessed!" And he ran his hand gently along the soft fur on the panting cat's back.

"Blessed be Allah! For surely it was Allah that sent thee to save me from that snake. It was a good fight. And thou art a brave warrior. Allah will reward thee for what thou hast done this day. From here on, thou shalt ever be the victor in any battle. No creature shall ever be able to throw a cat down on his back. Go in peace, Cat. Allah give thee long life!"

That is why, so the Arab storytellers say, even today a cat always lands upon his four feet.

Throw a cat down off a high rock! Throw him out of a tent! You will see that the blessing of the Prophet still works its magic. Never, never, never, does a cat fall on its back.

As for the Prophet's prayer for long life for the cat, who has not heard the saying "A cat has nine lives"?

The Cat Bride

Long, long ago when animals laughed and cried just like men, there once was a king who had many wives. His palace was in the faraway East Indian land of Kashmir. There, beyond the high mountains, it was the custom in those times for a king to take just as many wives as he liked.

The strange part of this story is not that this King had so many wives. No, it is that, with all his wives, this King did not have even one child. No son was there in his palace to gladden his heart. And no daughter either! And that is why this Kashmir King was so sad.

"Alas! Alas!" the King said every day. "Here I have all these wives. I feed them well. I give them fine clothes. Yet they bring me no children. I have no one to call me Father.

154

When I go away from this earth, who will remember me?"

One morning the King went into the zenana. This was the women's part of the palace. And there in the zenana, the King gathered his many wives, all together. They trembled as they stood around him, for his face was black with anger.

"Listen well, women," the King cried. "A child there must be, here in this palace. If no child is born within a year's time, out you all go. You shall go, every one of you, back to the families from whence you came. I will have no more to do with you."

The wives looked at each other sadly when their husband had left the zenana. Not one of them wanted to leave the King's palace. Life was pleasant there. They had good food to eat. They wore fine clothes. And they were happy together in their splendid zenana.

"We must pray to Shiva!" they said, and they fell on their knees before a small gilded statue of the Hindu god. They bumped their heads on the floor, and they prayed aloud.

"Give us a child, Shiva! Give us a child before the year is out! Or the King will send us away from his palace."

Each day the women sent up this prayer to Shiva. But the months went by, and no baby was born there in the zenana. Then came the very last day of the year.

"The last day of the year! And no child for the King! What shall we do?" the wives said to one another.

"We shall have to pretend a child has been born," said

the oldest wife of them all. Oh, that one truly was old. And she was wise. Everyone always asked her advice. Even the King asked her to foretell what would happen to him. He trusted her words even more than those of his wise sooth-sayers.

"A child, a girl child, has been born this day!"

This was the message the oldest wife sent to the King. It was not true. Yet it was not exactly a lie. For it happened that the favorite cat of the zenana had had kittens that day. And it was of a little white kitten they told the King when they said "a girl child has been born."

The King's heart was filled with joy at the news. So happy was he that he did not seem to mind when his oldest wife warned him not to look at the "baby."

"Bad luck will come to you and the child. Shiva came to me last night in a dream. He gave me the order that you were not to see the child until after she has been married." Thus the old wife frightened the King.

Now bad luck was the thing people in that land feared most in those long ago times. Like his people, this King believed firmly in luck and magic. Although he wanted badly to look upon the new baby, he obeyed his oldest wife's warning.

"How is it with my dear daughter?" the King often asked his wives in the zenana as the years went by.

"It is well with your daughter, O King!" the women replied. "Never was there a princess so beautiful. Happy and gay is she, and growing fast."

156

The King contented himself with these tales of the beauty and goodness of his fair daughter. And, of course, he was glad when the time came to think of her marriage. When she was married he would see her at last.

"Find a handsome young prince to be my daughter's husband!" the King said to his courtiers. "That Prince must be clever. He must be good, and he must have a kind heart. Tell him he shall have half of my kingdom when the marriage takes place."

The fine handsome young prince was found. The day of the wedding was set. Everybody was happy except the wives of the King.

What would happen now? Now, surely, the King would find out he had been tricked. Now he would know that the only daughter he had was a white cat. How angry would he be? These were the questions that were spoken in the zenana on the wedding day of the "princess."

It was the oldest wife who told them all what they must do.

"We shall tell the whole story to the kind-hearted Prince," she said. "We shall ask him to keep our secret until the marriage takes place. Perhaps he will willingly marry the cat for half our King's kingdom."

And that is how it happened. The frightened wives of the King told the bridegroom the whole story. Perhaps the young Prince's kind heart was touched by their tears. Or it just may have been that he thought also about his half of the kingdom.

157

Whatever made him do it, he did promise to go ahead with the wedding. And he promised never to tell the secret of his cat bride, not even to his own mother.

The marriage feast was splendid. It was a day of joy for everyone, even though no one saw the bride. Somehow or other, the oldest wife of the King persuaded him to let the bride's closed sedan chair be carried away without looking inside it.

"Your daughter is not truly married until she is at home in her new husband's palace," his old wife said to the King. "Do not risk your luck by being in too great a hurry. Wait just a little until you can visit your daughter in her new home."

It seems strange that the eager King should have agreed to such a thing. But then this whole story is strange.

The little cat bride was hidden from sight behind the curtains of her sedan chair. No one saw her as she was carried into the Prince's part of his father's palace.

"No one but me shall look upon my beautiful bride," the Prince gave the order. And he shut up the white cat in a special room.

All in the palace were disappointed. But they did not dare disobey the order of the young bridegroom. The Prince himself brought in the food for his bride. He gave her water to drink. He made her a bed on soft silken cushions.

The Prince treated the white cat with all the kindness of his good heart. Indeed, he loved her greatly. He felt that

158

there was something strange about his cat bride. Her eyes were big and soft, almost like those of a person. Sometimes the Prince thought the cat understood what he was saying to her. Sometimes it seemed as though she were laughing or crying.

You cannot blame the mother of this Prince for being curious about her son's bride. One day, when the Prince was away, the woman went to the door of the bride's room.

"I will just speak to my new daughter, and make her welcome," the Prince's mother said to herself. "Surely there can be no harm in my doing that."

She knocked lightly on the bride's door. But there was no answer. She thought she heard the sound of very soft footsteps. But no words came.

"Daughter, dear Daughter! Speak to me! I am your new mother," she called. "It is sad you must stay, always, shut up alone in that room. Shall I unlock the door? Will you walk in the garden? I will send everyone else away. You shall not be seen."

Still no words came from behind the bride's door. But there was a sound of soft weeping. This white cat was indeed almost like a true bride. Her cries touched the heart of the Prince's good mother.

The woman fell on her knees. She bowed her head to the floor. And she sent up a prayer to the Hindu goddess, Parvati, to Parvati, who was a wife of the great Shiva, himself.

"Have pity, Parvati, upon this poor bride!" the woman

prayed. "She must be lonely, that she cries so much. Soften the heart of my son, that he shall let her out of her prison."

Now the Kashmir folk said their Hindu gods had ways of knowing what took place on the earth. So they were sure that Parvati knew the true story of the Prince's young bride.

Parvati went to Shiva for help.

"Have mercy upon this poor little cat, Shiva," Parvati begged. "Have mercy upon this good young Prince who treats his cat bride so gently."

"I will have mercy upon them both," Shiva replied. "Go you, Parvati, to the room of the cat. In a silver bowl on her table you will find sweet-smelling oil for a bride's hair. Rub the oil into the cat's fur with your own hands. And she will become a bride fit for any prince."

Maybe Parvati found her way in by the window. Or she may have gone in through a keyhole. All things were possible to the old gods, so this story says.

However she did it, Parvati was there in the room with the cat. She found the magic bride's oil. And she rubbed it well into the soft white fur of the cat. At once, the white cat was changed into a princess, as fair as a silvery moon.

Parvati had rubbed the magic oil all over the cat's body, except for one tiny spot upon the left shoulder.

"This spot of fur we will leave. Then your Prince can be sure you are truly the bride whom he married," Parvati said to the girl. And truly, they say, there was always a tiny bit of soft cat fur on her left shoulder.

The goddess was wise. For when the Prince came home

and opened the door of the bride's room, he did not believe his own eyes. He marveled at the beauty of the princess he found there. Yet he did not forget his beloved cat bride.

"What have you done with my dear cat, Princess?" he cried.

"I am that cat," the girl answered him. But the Prince did not believe her until she had shown him the tiny bit of white cat fur upon her shoulder.

Then, oh, then, the Prince was happy. Now he could show his fair bride to his mother. Now all could know of her beauty and goodness.

No one was happier than the King, the bride's father, when he came to look upon his daughter at last.

"Parvati answered my prayers," the Prince's mother said to her son joyfully. "I prayed that Parvati would melt your selfish heart. I prayed you would let your dear bride come out into our zenana with the other women and girls."

The Prince never told his mother the magic secret of his cat bride. The wives of the King said not a word either. No one except this storyteller knew that the beautiful Princess had once been a white cat.

The Ghost Dog of
South Mountain

People who lived on the South Mountain of the Blue Ridge often saw the black Ghost Dog. At least, they said they had seen it. And they told many stories about their meetings with the strange beast.

They told how the Ghost Dog always appeared on the road that led to the Rich Woman's house. How it stood in the way and would not let a man pass. How no horse would go on until the black dog-shape melted away into the evening dark.

"I met the Ghost Dog once on a path near the Rich Woman's house," one farmer said to his neighbors. "It was after the sunset. But the stars were out. And I saw the dog clearly.

"Bigger than any live dog, he was. With a red tongue

and long white teeth. Right in the path, the dog stood. He would not move out of my way. It was lucky I had a staff in my hand. I beat the Ghost Dog with that staff, or he would have jumped at me."

"Did you harm the Ghost Dog?" the neighbors asked.

"How could I harm a ghost dog?" the farmer answered. "A ghost dog, that's what this one surely is. No live dog was there at all. My staff met only air when it fell on his head. Yet I saw that big black dog with my own eyes."

"I once shot at the Ghost Dog of South Mountain," another man declared. "He stood there before me, coal black, and with eyes that burned like fire in the dark. I could never have missed him. He was close to my gun. But my shot went right through him. The dog did not move. It was me that turned back. It was me that ran away."

Oh, everyone along that part of the Blue Ridge knew it was bad luck to meet this ghost of a dog. Most of them knew it was better to turn and run away from it. Old Jerry, who sometimes drank far too much, learned this to his hurt.

Jerry was riding his old horse up the mountain from the town in the lowland. Suddenly his horse stopped short. There ahead in the narrow road stood the Ghost Dog.

If Jerry had not had too much to drink, he would have known better. But he called to his horse, "Get along! Get along there!" And he brought his whip sharply down upon the old horse's back.

Jerry's old horse would not take one single step nearer

the Ghost Dog. His master shouted at him. The man swung his whip once again.

Instead of going ahead, the old horse started to back down the mountain. He snorted with fear. Then he reared up on his hind legs. He was like a young colt.

That horse threw Old Jerry off his back, and he ran away down the mountain road. A broken leg was what Jerry got for his foolishness. Yes, that's what Jerry got for trying to force his horse to ride at the Ghost Dog.

Many people on South Mountain tried to explain the black Ghost Dog. Granny S. always said she knew the true story. And this is her tale, which I have here for you.

Granny S. should have known. She lived on South Mountain for one hundred years. And she had seen the Rich Woman with her own eyes.

The Rich Woman may have had another name once. But the "Rich Woman" was what they called her in all the log cabins along the Blue Ridge. This was because she was so much richer than anyone else on the Ridge.

The Rich Woman had a fine stone house on the side of the mountain. Why such a rich woman should choose to live there in that lonely place, Granny S. never told me.

She must have been rich to have paid men to clear so much rough mountain land. There were green fields around her stone house. She had a big garden, a grape arbor, and an orchard filled with apple and peach trees.

Sheep grazed on the land of the Rich Woman. Cows

gave her milk and yellow cream. The little house over her cool flowing spring of water was filled with her milk bowls.

Good fortune seemed to follow that Rich Woman. Her sheep all had twin lambs. Her cows never lost their calves. She sold her apples and peaches for a great deal of money.

What she did with the money, nobody knew. No one ever heard of her spending an extra penny on herself or her two sons.

Where was the husband of the Rich Woman? Granny S. did not say much about him. But she told of the woman's two sons who grew up in that fine stone house.

One of these was the good-tempered lad, Adam, whom everyone loved. The other was Ethan, whom everyone hated.

Adam had always a pleasant "Good morning" for whomever he met on the mountain road. It was good to come up with that smiling young man, and his gentle black dog.

In those days the black dog on South Mountain was a live dog. He was a friendly, playful puppy, capering about at the heels of his master, the pleasant youth, Adam.

With Ethan it was different. Ethan walked, or rode, all by himself. And always he took more than his half of the road. Without a smile or an "Excuse me" he crowded all he met off to one side.

Ethan had no smiles for his good brother, either. They said on South Mountain that Ethan hated Adam. They said Ethan's black hate was what drove Adam away from his mother's house.

166

The Rich Woman cried when Adam went off to seek his fortune on the other side of the Blue Ridge. The neighbors were sorry, too. But saddest of all was Adam's black dog that had to be left behind.

The dog moped and whined. He lay on the doorstep of the stone house. Always, he was looking far down the road to see if his dear master was coming back.

Adam's dog took good care to keep out of the way of the bad-tempered Ethan. The dog knew the hurt of a kick from Ethan's boot, and of a blow from his staff.

The Rich Woman was kind to the black dog, and the dog took to following her about the place. All the day long he walked by her side. All night he slept at the foot of her bed. Into the garden, out in the barn, over the fields, and into the forest, that black dog went about with the Rich Woman.

At last one day, the Rich Woman felt that her end was not far off. And before she died she wrote down her last wishes on paper. With her pen and strong black ink she wrote, so her words could not be changed.

"My lands shall belong to my two sons. The stone house shall be theirs. But my money shall belong to whichever one of my sons it is that finds it." This was the will the Rich Woman left.

Hard-hearted Ethan was secretly glad when his mother was dead.

"Her lands and her house shall be all mine," he said to himself, "for I shall not tell my brother that our mother

167

is dead. It will be a long time before Adam learns of her will. I shall have the first chance to look for her money."

Ethan searched the stone house. He looked all through the cellar. He poked around in the attic. He took up the floor boards. He pulled down the walls of the closets. Indeed, that young man almost tore the stone house to pieces. But he found no treasure.

Ethan was so busy looking for the money that he let the farm work go. There were weeds in the garden. Bugs ruined the fruit. There were no apples or peaches for him to sell.

No money came in now to buy new seeds for the next year. There was not enough food for the farm animals. One by one he sold them, the sheep and the cows, the horses and the pigs.

"I would sell you too, Dog," Ethan said to his brother's pet. "But no one would buy you."

The poor dog was thin. He had grown weak because Ethan gave him so little to eat. The black dog lived on rabbits and other small creatures he could catch in the woods. Soon he was almost too weak to run after them.

"Get out of my way," Ethan cried one day in going out of the door. "I am sick of your whining." That wicked young man gave the black dog such a blow with his stick that the poor creature died.

"Now at last Adam's dog will be gone from my sight," Ethan said as he buried the dog's body out in the garden.

But he was wrong. That very night, the black dog came into the room where Ethan was going to sleep. From his bed, the man could see the dog standing there, big and black, right in the doorway.

Each night just after sunset, the Ghost Dog would appear. His eyes burned like two red-hot coals of fire. His long tongue was red between his white teeth. Wherever Ethan went after dark, the Ghost Dog was close behind him.

The young man could not rest. All day long he thought of the coming night and how the black Ghost Dog would look at him. At last there was nothing for him to do but go away from the stone house.

"I have looked for my mother's treasure all through this house," Ethan said to the neighbors. "I have looked in the barns. I have even looked under the trough in the pigsty.

"It may be my mother had no money at all, though what she did with all she had I cannot guess. But I am going away from here. So long as the Ghost Dog roams through the stone house, I cannot live here. My brother is welcome to this gloomy place. May he be just as unhappy here as I have been!"

The very next day Ethan packed up everything he could take with him. He went far, far away, and no one ever saw that bad-tempered young man on South Mountain again.

It was just after Ethan left that the cabin folk began to meet the black Ghost Dog on the roads near the stone house.

"The Ghost Dog is looking for someone," they said. "He surely is watching for his master to come home again."

They were right. It was Adam for whom the Ghost Dog

169

was waiting. Adam himself told Granny S. just how it was.

Somehow word of his mother's death went out over the mountains. In spite of Ethan, Adam heard the news. He learned that his brother had nearly torn the stone house to pieces in looking for their mother's treasure. And Adam thought he would just go back and see it all for himself.

On a table in the stone house, Adam found the paper which his mother had written upon. This was her will that said, "My money shall belong to the one of my sons who finds it."

Ethan had left Adam a paper too. His paper said, "If you ever come back, this place is all yours. I want no part of it."

The very first evening, Adam was sitting by the table looking at the two papers. Something, or someone, made him look toward the door. There he saw his black dog, wagging his tail.

"Black Boy! Come here!" the young man called out. The Ghost Dog was so real that Adam thought at first it must be alive. But when he laid his hand on the dog's head, he could feel nothing. And his neighbors had already told him how his black dog had died.

Adam saw the Ghost Dog run to the door, then look back at him. When the young man did not rise to follow, the dog ran back again to his side. Again he ran to the door. Again he looked back as if to beg his master to come with him.

So Adam got up and went after his dog out into the moonlight. The dog led him past the barn, through the

apple orchard, and into the woods. There, before a small pile of rocks, the Ghost Dog came to a stop. The eerie animal poked his black nose into a hole at the bottom of the pile.

Adam reached into the hole with his stick. There was a ringing sound, as if the stick had touched metal. Then, one after the other, the young man laid the stones aside.

Before his eyes there lay a great metal box. What there was in it you have already guessed, I am sure. Yes, that great box was full of bright golden coins. In it was the treasure which his mother had hidden, and it was a rich treasure.

Granny S. always said that the Rich Woman wanted her son Adam to have her money. Why else would she have shown the black dog where she hid it?

Granny S. said too that the reason Adam would not live in the stone house was his brother, Ethan. He was afraid Ethan would want to come back and live there with him.

Whatever his reason was, Adam sold his mother's farm on the mountainside. He went back to the lands beyond the Blue Ridge. And his neighbors on South Mountain never saw him again.

Do you think the Ghost Dog went away with his master? Or was it that he now could rest easy in his grave under the apple tree? His work was well done. He had led his master to the treasure out in the woods.

In any case, no one today ever meets the black Ghost Dog on the paths of South Mountain there in the Blue Ridge.

The Little
Lion Dog and
the Blind Prince

A thousand and a thousand years ago, a huge lion fell in love with a tiny monkey. At least that is the way they say it happened, in China.

The lion was a great tawny beast. And the monkey was a small, dainty, brown marmoset with bright darting eyes and amusing ways.

"How should I marry an enormous creature like you?" the little marmoset laughed at the very idea. "It is true, Lion, that you are the most splendid of all beasts, and I could love you well. But even one gentle pat from your great paw would squash me flat as a bo leaf. No, I must marry a beast more my own size."

173

But the lion did not give up. Instead he went off to find Buddha, the Wise One, who could work magic.

"Master! Master!" he begged, "Make me as small as my dear marmoset. My heart bursts with love for that charming creature. But she only will marry a beast her own size."

"How shall a King of the Beasts be content to be so small?" Buddha demanded. "How shall you kill your prey, Lion, if you are no bigger than a marmoset?"

"Let the other lions be kings!" the lovesick animal cried. "If I may wed my beloved, I shall be satisfied to kill just the very small creatures, such as chipmunks and mice."

Buddha was touched by such great love in the lion's heart. He laid his hand on the shaggy yellow head, and straightway the lion began to shrink. Smaller and smaller he grew, until at last he was only a little bigger than the marmoset.

The two then were married, the lion and the monkey. And they lived happily together, always loving each other.

The curious children they brought into the world were like both of these parents. Shaggy gold-colored manes hung on their strong little necks. Like their lion father, too, they washed their faces with soft tufted paws. They had the lion's loving heart, and his bold courage.

Their bright darting eyes and their short stubby noses made one think of their mother, the wee marmoset. They had her dainty ways, and their wide grinning mouths told that, like her, they loved fun and playing tricks.

Yet these baby beasts were not lion cubs. They were not

174

true monkeys either. The Chinese declare they were the very first little "lion dogs" which we call Pekingese.

A wise little lion dog named Fu and a blind prince named Ming Cho are the heroes of this tale. Cho was the son of the Emperor, Ming Ti; and Fu also lived with that proud emperor in his splendid palace.

"Palace dogs" is another Chinese name for Pekingese. They were the favorite royal pets, and none but an emperor was allowed to possess them.

The little lion dogs ran where they would through the palaces. They slept on silken cushions, and they dined on white rice and sharks' fins, on birds' livers and breasts of quail.

Whenever Ming Ti entered his throne room, two wee gold-colored lion dogs marched ahead, barking "Make way! Make way! The Son of Heaven comes!" Two others walked close behind, carrying the hem of the Emperor's yellow silk robe between their white teeth.

Ming Ti loved his lion dogs almost as well as his own children. And of all his sons, the boy, Cho, was dearest to his proud heart. Cho was the strongest. Cho was the handsomest. Cho was the best at swimming and riding. Besides, Cho already could write with the rabbit-hair brush. He could read all the picture writings on the silk banners that hung on the palace walls.

All was well with Ming Cho until the great storm, when the wind blew so hard that yellow tiles flew off the palace roofs. The sky was black as night. Lightning flashed. Thun-

der roared. And a giant thunderbolt hurled itself down out
of the clouds.

The ball of lightning fell so close to Ming Cho that he
was knocked flat on the garden path. When they picked the
boy up, he still was alive, but the bright glare of the fiery
ball had blinded his eyes.

One would think such misfortune would make a father's
heart only more loving toward his dearest son. But it was
not so with Ming Ti.

"Keep that blind son of mine out of my way!" the proud
emperor ordered. "I cannot bear to hear him tapping his
way about with his stick."

It was then that the little gold-colored lion dog, Fu,
became Prince Cho's guide and friend. On the end of a
silver chain, the clever dog led his young master safely and
surely all through the palace. Fu guided Cho out into the
gardens and down to the river in which the boy loved so to
swim.

The little dog often swam ahead of his master through
the swift water. He even learned to lead the pony on which
Cho used to ride. With the bridle reins held tight between
his teeth, Fu walked ahead whenever Cho rode out through
the palace gate into the city.

With Fu to guide his steps, Cho made no noise now to
disturb his selfish father. But Ming Ti was not satisfied.
He was ashamed to have anyone know that he, the Son
of Heaven, had a blind son.

"Send Cho away from here," Ming Ti ordered at last.

176

"Set him down in the faraway forest where he cannot find his way home again!" Secretly the cruel emperor hoped a tiger from the north would end the life of his son.

Cho wept. So did the palace guards, all of whom loved the boy. But it was the warm soft tongue of Fu, licking his hand, that brought comfort to Cho.

"Perhaps they will let you go along with me, Fu?" Cho said aloud.

"Indeed, Fu shall go with you, and you also shall have your pony to ride upon," the palace guards cried.

"Do not fear, my dear master!" Fu said as they went together out into the wide world. (People declared then that lion dogs talked with human voices. They said that they laughed like children and that they wept real tears.)

"Each day, with my tricks, I will earn money for our food," Fu said. "Each night I will lead you to a safe shelter."

Earning money was easy for this little dog with the lion's heart. In every village people crowded about the gold-colored palace dog and the pony who carried the blind prince on his back. Then Fu went through all his tricks.

First he rolled over and over, like a furry gold ball. Next he played dead. Most amusing of all, he made kowtows to the crowd. Fu tucked his little short forelegs into a kneeling position, and he bumped his proud shaggy head three times on the ground. Truly, it was just as if he were kowtowing to the Emperor, Ming Ti.

How the crowd laughed! When Fu next sat up on his

177

haunches to beg, they dropped copper coins on the ground before him. Often there were enough coppers to buy hot rice and fish, or even a bit of sweet juicy pork.

At night Fu led the way to a shady tree or some other safe shelter. And it was under such a tree that the Good Stranger came to find them.

Perhaps it was all a dream. Or perhaps by some magic the blind prince and his dog actually met the man. Perhaps the old pony saw the Good Stranger too, for he raised his head from eating the green grass under the tree, and he looked and he looked.

"It must be some good spirit," Cho cried to Fu. Somehow he could feel that this was no ordinary traveler.

"Perhaps it is the Wise Buddha, himself," the lion dog whispered.

"Alas, I cannot see you, Honorable Sir," Cho sadly said. "To my great sorrow, my eyes are without light."

"You need not be blind, Ming Cho," the Good Stranger spoke kindly. "Good deeds can bring the light back into your eyes. Each time you help others, your darkness shall grow less."

Cho dropped down on his knees to kowtow his thanks, but the Stranger was speaking once more.

"Take care, Ming Cho! As good deeds shall bring you light, so bad deeds shall take the light away." Then he was gone.

Next morning Cho talked with Fu about the Good Stranger. But the day was hot, and their road was rough.

178

Somehow no one seemed to want to pay Fu for his tricks. Only one copper coin did they have for buying their supper.

Cho was just thinking how hungry he was, when they met a beggar outside the wall of a town.

"I am blind. I am lame. I am very hungry. O Master, give me a copper!" the beggar called out to Cho when he heard the sound of the pony's hoofs on the hard road.

"I am blind, too," Cho answered. "Only one copper coin have I left. It must buy supper for myself, and also for my dog and my pony."

"Ai-ya! You have a dog for a friend. You have a pony to ride upon. And you are not old and lame," the beggar whined.

"Truly you need this copper more than I." The young prince felt sorry for the old beggar, and he handed him the coin.

At once, to his great surprise, Cho saw a faint light before his blind eyes.

"I see light, Fu!" the excited boy called out to his dog. "Truly I do see light."

"Surely, surely, our stranger of last night was the Good Buddha," the lion dog cried. "Buddha knows all things. Your good deed has brought you light."

Next day they met an old woman hobbling along on aching bound feet. As was the ancient Chinese custom then, her toes were tied tightly under her soles so as to make her feet tiny. Every step hurt. She could scarcely walk.

"You shall ride on my pony, Honorable Grandmother,"

said the good-hearted Cho. "My dog shall go before you, and I will walk at your side, holding my pony's mane."

The Prince had not taken two steps before the light in his eyes was brighter than before. Faintly, now, he could see the shape of his little lion dog walking ahead, with the pony's reins in his mouth.

But sometimes Cho forgot the words of the Good Stranger. It was like that when he felt the string of prayer beads roll under his foot on the highway near the gate of the city. By the soft soapy touch of the beads he picked up, he knew they were made of the precious stone, jade.

"Jade beads bring much money," Cho said to Fu. "I shall sell these in the city. Then we shall have plenty to eat and a bed to sleep upon."

"The beads are not yours to sell, Master," the little lion dog growled. But the Prince did not listen. He was about to hand over the prayer beads to a merchant in the Street of Jade, when he noticed that the light in his eyes was beginning to fade. Just in time he remembered the Good Stranger's warning. He snatched back the beads and he mounted his pony.

"Take me back to the city gate, Fu!" he called out. "It was only our hunger that tempted me to do wrong."

There he found the servants of a rich man looking and looking for the lost beads. The silver coins they gave Cho as a reward bought a fine supper, and also a bed for the night.

Best of all, next day Cho found that now he could see

dimly both houses and people. He could even make out a boat floating on the river. Although the boy did not know it, this was the very river near his father's palace. The little dog, Fu, had cleverly brought him close to his old home.

There was a man in the boat, and that man was in trouble. His oars had been swept away, and his boat was whirled round and round by the swift water. Suddenly the little boat overturned. The man was thrown into the river, and he was shouting "Help! Help!"

"He cannot swim, Fu," Cho cried. "Ho, there, man, hold on tight to the side of your boat. We will try to get help."

Fu barked and Cho called, and many people came running. But not one was willing to swim the swift river to save the man's life.

"I am only a boy," Cho said to the crowd. "I am not strong enough to bring the man to land by myself. I am almost blind, but I have my brave little lion dog to guide me. And we can both swim. We will take a rope to that poor man; then, together, you others can pull him safely ashore."

The crowd held their breaths while the blind prince and the golden dog fought their way through the rushing river. The drowning man had lost his hold on the boat. The crowd cheered when Cho tied the rope round him and gave the signal to pull.

Panting, the boy and the dog flung themselves out again on the bank of the river. They were even more tired than the man they had saved.

182

"Ai! Ai! This man is the Son of Heaven, himself. He is the Emperor, Ming Ti," the crowd whispered, one to another. "Whatever was the Son of Heaven doing in a boat all by himself?"

"Ai! Ai!" Now it was the Emperor speaking as he looked down on the two who had saved him from the river. "This is Cho, my own son, whom I used so badly. And this is our lion dog, Fu, who is well named 'Good Luck'!"

"Cho, my dear son," the Emperor was weeping now. "I have been a bad father, and I beg you to forgive me. Come back again to your home, and all shall do you honor."

But the Prince could not easily forget his hard journey from the faraway forest. Anger still filled his heart. He was about to refuse the forgiveness his father asked of him, when he saw his small golden lion dog sit up on his hind legs. Fu gave a soft bark. "Be kind, Ming Cho, be kind!" he whimpered, and the boy's heart grew soft.

"I forgive you, Honorable Father, I will come home." Cho kowtowed like any other dutiful son. When he raised his head once again, he gave a happy cry. His act of forgiveness had taken away the very last of his blindness.

"I see!" Ming Cho cried. "Now I see clearly the face of my father, and I see the loving eyes of my dear Fu who guided me so faithfully in my time of darkness."

The boy gathered the little lion dog into his arms, and together they rode on the pony, back to their old happy life in the palace of the Emperor Ming Ti.

183

The Cat
of Bubastis

"Never, never, never harm a cat!" Grandmothers used to say this in long-ago Egypt.

"The gods will be angry if you do not treat cats kindly," they warned their grandchildren. "Bad luck will come to you if you are unkind to a cat. If the gods do not punish you, then our King will."

In those days in Egypt the cat was a god. Men had even been put to death for killing a cat.

Some say that Egypt was the earliest home of the cat. They say the very first pet pussy was an African wild cat which found its way into a house on the banks of the Nile River.

"The cat is the child of the sun," the old Egyptians used to declare. "Watch how the cat loves to lie in the sun. Even the fierce noonday heat of the sun is not too hot for a cat. That is why our Sky Goddess, Bast, has the head of a cat."

In many old Egyptian homes, a small statue of this cat-headed goddess stood in a place of honor. Many people said their prayers to Bast.

There were statues and paintings of other animals, too, in old Egyptian temples. But at the time of this story none was half so important as the cat.

On an island in the River Nile a fine city was built to honor the Cat Goddess. Bubastis, "Home of Bast," was the name of this city. And it was the capital of all the land.

Great temples were built there in Bubastis. Today, thousands of years later, those temples have fallen apart. But one can still see their splendid pillars, and their carved walls.

People came to Bubastis from all parts of Egypt. They bent their heads low, and they said prayers before the statues and paintings of the tall slender goddess with the cat's head.

There was even a cat cemetery in old Bubastis. Here, in holes cut into rocks, hundreds of cat mummies were placed in rows. The rich wrapped their dead pussies in fine linen cloth. They put them into wood mummy cases. Like the Egyptian kings and queens, the dead cats had their likenesses painted on the outside of their mummy cases.

The curious tale I am about to tell you comes from this cat city of old Bubastis. You can believe it or not, just as you like. But the old Egyptian books say it truly happened, just as I tell it here.

It was time for the great spring festival in Bubastis. From all over Egypt hundreds of thousands of people were hurrying toward Bast's splendid city. From near and from far they came to do honor to the Cat Goddess.

Some walked many miles over the land. Some rode upon donkeys. The rich traveled in chairs, carried by men.

More came by water, moving up or down the River Nile. Flat-bottomed boats floated down, down the great river. Other boats of the same kind came up the stream from the cities along the sea.

How many boats there were upon the Nile on this day! Their huge bird-wing sails rose high into the air. The men at their oars pulled hard as they rowed to help the boats move along faster.

So many boats were there near Bubastis that one could never have counted them all. So close were they to each other that people could talk from one deck to another.

A handsome youth, Kebo, was standing on the high deck of one of the river boats. Kebo was the son of a rich father. He traveled in great comfort upon this fine boat to the feast of Bast.

It was to another fine boat, moving along beside his, that the young man, Kebo, kept turning his eyes. Upon that boat he had spied a beautiful young girl. She was more beautiful, he thought, than any other girl in the world.

"Neither the moon in her silver splendor, nor the sun in his golden glory, has such shining beauty as this girl," Kebo said to himself. "Her eyes are bright as the stars. Her smile is sweet as new honey. She moves with the grace of a flower in a summer breeze."

186

Truly the girl was fair to look upon. In Egyptian fashion her big eyes were outlined with black paint. Her lips and her cheeks were colored rosy red. There was red on her fingernails and on her toenails, as well.

Her robes were of fine linen. Her earrings, her necklace, and her arm bands all were of gold. It was clear that this girl and her mother, who sat beside her on the boat deck, were members of an important family of old Egypt.

It was not strange then that Kebo should fall in love with this girl at very first sight. At once, in his heart, he knew that he wanted her for his bride.

The girl could not help noticing the young man who gazed at her so lovingly. Kebo, himself, was good to look upon. The youth stood tall and straight. His head was carried proudly. His shoulders were broad. And his eyes were kind. The girl could not help smiling back at the handsome young man on the boat next to hers.

Both sails and oars were being used to send the flat boats along the river that day. All wanted to make haste. Everyone was eager to reach the festival city as quickly as might be.

Suddenly a cry was heard from Kebo's boat. "Look! There in the river! On that bit of wood, floating! There is a young kitten."

"It is a sign of bad luck," the people said to each other. "A cat must not be drowned on Bast's own feast day."

"Stop the boats! Stop the boats! The kitten will be struck

by one of the oars. Or a crocodile will swallow it!" Everyone
was shouting advice as to how to save the little cat.

But the boats were going too fast. Kebo saw at once that
they could not stop in time. He threw off his fine linen robe.
And he dived into the Nile waters.

There were cheers from all decks as the youth swam toward the bit of floating wood. There were more cheers
when he held the kitten up out of the water. They threw
him a rope so that he could climb back onto the boat. And
everyone cheered again.

"The little cat will surely bring us good luck. It shall be
our mascot," the boat's captain said. And he set out a meal
of Nile fish for the kitten.

Indeed, the best of good luck seemed to go with the boat
after that. The wind seemed to push against its sails harder.
The sun seemed to put more strength into the arms of the
oarsmen. Faster and faster Kebo's boat went along on the
river.

Kebo's boat soon pulled ahead of all the other boats near
it. But this, the youth thought, was not good luck at all. It
was bad luck for him. For the boat of his fair lady was now
far behind him. She was lost to his sight in the throng of
other boats.

"Surely my lady is on her way to Bast's festival," Kebo
said to himself. "Surely she will end her journey at Bubastis.
I shall wait for her at the boat landing. I shall follow her to
her stopping place. Thus I shall find out who she is, and
I can then ask for her as my bride."

Kebo's boat tied up at the landing, and the young man stood there waiting for his lady's boat to arrive. He watched and he watched. But when her boat came into sight at last, it sailed on beyond him. It came in to land at a different, and faraway, part of the city.

As fast as he could, the young man made his way through the festival crowds. There were so many people on the streets of Bubastis that day that he could not go very fast.

When at last Kebo reached the other boat landing, his fair lady's boat was already tied up. And she was already gone. No one could tell him who she was, or where she could be found.

"What shall I do now?" Kebo said to himself with a heavy heart. "I cannot rest until I see my fair lady again. But how shall I find her among these thousands of people?"

How indeed could anyone be found in such a great crowd? Singing and dancing, the merrymakers filled the streets. Kebo pushed his way through them, looking and looking for the girl from the boat. No matter how gaily drums beat, nor how sweetly flutes played, he never stopped looking for her.

Now and again he met bands of girls dancing. Their bare feet kept time to the clicking of small ivory shells which they held high over their heads. People, watching, sang with the dancing girls. They clapped their hands in time to the music of the flutes and the drums.

Kebo looked hard at each group. Then he hurried along.

For nowhere did he find the fair face and sweet smile for which he was looking.

At last the sun was dropping low in the sky. And Kebo was tired with pushing through the crowds.

"I will rest in Bast's temple for a little while," he decided. "There I will pray to the Cat Goddess. Perhaps she will help me as I helped her little cat out of the river today."

Before the stone statue of Bast, the young man bowed down. He held his arms out in front of him, and he prayed, "O Lady of Life! O Goddess of the Sky! Help me find my dear bride! Help me, Great Bast!"

When he had ended his prayer, Kebo raised his head. He looked up into the stone face of the Cat Goddess. To his surprise the eyes of the goddess seemed to be alive.

"Her eyes move!" Kebo cried aloud. "Her lips part in a smile. Surely, oh, surely she answers my prayer."

At that very moment, the youth felt a soft touch on his leg. He looked down, and, lo, there was a cat. It was a big cat, a great yellow cat. It was a splendid cat with long legs, just like those of the cats in the paintings of Bast on the temple walls.

The yellow cat held its head high and proud, like the cat's head on the statue before him. With one quiet "Miaou" the cat turned about. With slow even pace, it walked to the temple steps. There it turned around and looked back at Kebo, as if expecting him to follow.

"It was as if someone pulled me by the hand," Kebo told

the tale later. "It was as if something told me to follow that cat."

Down the temple steps, through the merry festival crowds, they walked. First the cat. Then the handsome young man.

Once or twice Kebo lost sight of the yellow cat. But soon he felt again the soft touch of the animal rubbing against his bare leg. So the two of them walked through the streets of Bubastis.

At last, at the door of a very fine house, the yellow cat stopped. Sounds of music and dancing came from within.

The young man feared to enter, lest he should not be welcomed. He stood there alone, wondering about the cat and this house. Then the door opened. And there was the fair lady he had been seeking. The yellow cat had led him to her dwelling place.

When the girl saw Kebo, she smiled more sweetly even than before. And she said to those with her, "Here he is. This is the brave young man I was telling about. It was he who saved the life of the kitten that had fallen into the Nile."

After that all went well. A rich handsome young man like Kebo was a fit bridegroom for any girl in that land. He asked for his lady's hand in marriage in the proper way. And not so very long after that, she became his true bride.

What became of the yellow cat from Bast's temple? I do not know. But you may be sure Kebo and his bride never forgot her.

Among all the rich wedding gifts, there was one that pleased the bride above all the others. It was a tiny thing, a small good-luck charm. Kebo had had a jeweler make it from a bit of the clear yellow stone, jasper. It had the shape of a proud yellow cat. Indeed, it was exactly like the temple cat of Bubastis.

The Boy
Who Had to Draw
Cats

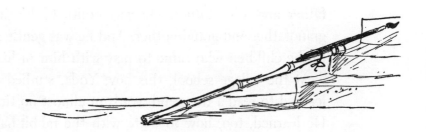

Long ago, in Japan, people say there was an artist more famous than any other. With his brushes, fine as a hair, and his colors soft as a rainbow, he painted beautiful pictures.

Some showed spring blossoms so real you would think you could smell their perfume. Some were of country roads along which you almost thought you were walking.

But the pictures this artist liked best to make were pictures of cats. Big cats and little cats! Sleeping cats and fighting cats! The walls of his home in the old city of Kyoto were covered with cats.

A strange story is told in Japan about this ancient painter of cats. Some say the tale could not be true. Others say anything could happen in those long-ago times. You can decide for yourself. Here is the tale—

No one remembers this artist's name now. Perhaps this is because he was known everywhere as the "Painter of Cats." We may as well call him Yoda. That is a good enough name for a boy. And it was when he was a boy—a very small boy—that Yoda began to make pictures of cats.

Yoda was a good boy. He always bowed low before his father and his mother. He was polite to his honorable grandfather and grandmother. And he was gentle and kind to the children who came to play with him in his garden.

At the village school, this boy, Yoda, studied well. He learned to read a thousand words in almost no time at all. He learned, too, how to write with the rabbit-hair brush. With its tiny soft point he made the fine lines of the Japanese word-pictures. Indeed, the word-pictures made by Yoda's brush were finer than those of any other boy in the school.

"Yoda truly is a good boy," everyone said. But then they always added with a sigh, "If only Yoda did not like so well to draw cats."

You see, ever since that boy put his first brush into the ink-paste, he had made pictures of cats. On each bit of paper he got his hands on, he drew with his brush a black and white cat. When there was no paper, as often as not he would draw cats on the walls. He even drew cats on the kimonos he wore.

"Why? Why, my son, do you spoil the walls of our house with your rabbit-hair brush? Why do you spoil the very clothes you wear with your inky cats?" His mother almost wept.

"I do not know, Mother," the boy answered. "I truly do not know. A spirit must get into my fingers. I just have to draw cats."

At the school in the village, it was the same story.

"Yoda truly is a good boy," his teachers said. "But he draws cats when he should be learning to make new words with his brush. We give him clean paper. He brushes his words well. But always in the corner of the paper he draws a cat. So the lesson is spoiled."

It made no difference at all to his family and his teachers that Yoda drew very good cats. They said cats did not belong on his school papers, or on the walls of his house.

One day Yoda's mother found a long line of cats painted on the fine white straw matting that covered her floor. Then, indeed, she was angry.

"On the walls, on his clothes, and now on our fine matting, our son has drawn cats," she said to the boy's father. "Yoda is a big boy now. He is old enough to know better. Let us send him to dwell with the good priests in the temple. Perhaps they will be able to cure him of drawing cats."

So Yoda went off to the temple school. The yellow-robed priests of the Great Buddha were kind. They taught the boy well, and he tried hard to please them.

All went well until the priests began to find the cats which Yoda could not help drawing. They found Yoda's cats on the books the boy studied from. They found his cats on the corners of the temple writings that hung on the wall in the great hall. And they were not pleased at all.

They scolded Yoda. They punished him. But he did not stop making pictures of cats with his brush and his ink-paste.

"You will never be anything else but an artist," the head priest said to Yoda. The old man shook his head sadly. "We do not teach artists in this temple. We wish you well, but you do not belong in our school."

The good priests gave Yoda a bag of rice for his journey home. But the youth did not go home. He did not dare tell his father that the priests would not keep him in this temple school. He knew his father would be angry that his son was still drawing cats.

"Perhaps some other temple school will take me in," the youth thought. He walked on and on across the valley, and over the paths on the mountains.

As the sun dropped low in the sky, Yoda hoped he could find some kind of shelter for the night. And at last he came to a lonely temple, beyond a small village.

There was no light in the temple. No sound was to be heard. No priest was in sight.

"Where can the priests be?" Yoda asked himself. "Why are the twigs and the leaves not swept away from the temple floors?"

"Well," the youth said aloud, "I will clean out the great hall. The priests will be pleased when they come back.

198

Perhaps then they will take me in and let me live here
with them."

He found a broom in one corner, and he swept the floor
clean. He pulled the cobwebs down from the high corners.
And, since it was growing dark, he lit the temple lanterns.

"It would do no harm at all," Yoda thought, "if I drew
just one cat here on the wall." He got out his beloved brush
and he wet his ink-cake.

Yoda drew one cat. Then another cat, and another. It
came into his mind to draw some very fierce cats. So he
drew them snarling and spitting. The cats were so lifelike
that Yoda himself was almost afraid of them.

"I think I will not sleep out here in this great hall with
those angry cats," the youth thought. So he crept into a
small room just off the big hall. He put out the temple
lights, and he went off to sleep.

It was not long, however, before Yoda was waked by
many strange noises. His hair stood on end at the sound of
the shrill screams and the angry snarls. It was as if giants
were fighting in the great hall of the temple. Yoda did not
dare even to look to see what was happening there.

When morning came, the lonely temple was quiet again.
Yoda could not have said when the noises had stopped. At
some time or other he had dropped off to sleep again. Now
the morning sun was shining into his little room.

"I will ring the bell for the sunrise, for the good priests,"
the youth said to himself. He knew the ways of a temple
from his life with the other yellow-clad ones.

199

Yoda stood still for a moment to listen to the sweet notes of the bell, floating out over the valley. Then he turned to the great hall.

What a sight he saw there! Lanterns and tables were overturned. The floor was covered with blood. And lying there before him was the dead body of a rat, almost as big as a man.

"What is this?" Yoda cried aloud. "Who has been here? What brave man has killed this giant rat?"

The youth looked about him. And he gave a loud cry. There was blood on the mouth of every one of the cats he had drawn on the temple wall!

"It was my own cats, come to life!" Yoda cried out. "It was my cats who killed the Giant Rat." He stood open-mouthed in wonder.

Just then the Head Man of the nearby village came up the steps of the temple.

"Who rang the temple bell?" he demanded of Yoda, who stood in the door. "The priests did not ring it. They have long been gone from this place. Who are you who has dared to spend the night here?"

"I am called Yoda," the youth answered, making a bow before the village Head Man. "I needed shelter for the night. I saw no harm in sleeping here in the temple."

"But did you not see the Rat?" the village Head Man cried in amazement. "Did you not have a visit from the Giant Rat? It was that rat that drove all our good priests away from the temple."

Yoda hardly dared tell the man what had happened. He was afraid he would never believe the strange story. But he led the Head Man into the great hall of the temple, to see for himself.

"You have killed the Giant Rat! That will be good news for our valley." The Head Man was joyful.

"Nay, it was not I," Yoda answered. "It was my cats."

He told the strange tale all the way from the beginning. How from his childhood he had liked to draw cats with his rabbit-hair brush. How he drew cats and drew cats. How he could not help drawing cats. And how last night he had drawn the fighting cats on the walls of this lonely temple.

"You can see, Honorable Sir," Yoda said to the Head Man, "by the rat's blood still on their mouths, you can tell it was my cats, come alive, that killed the Giant Rat."

The Head Man shook his head. He never had seen drawings of cats that looked so alive. Surely some spirit lived in this youth's clever fingers.

"However it was," the Head Man said to Yoda, "you have freed our valley from the Giant Rat, who has been eating our rice. Our children now will be safe from his teeth. We can sleep now at night without fear of the rat."

"Your cats do look alive, young man. Indeed they look as though they could kill one thousand rats. You, my young artist, will one day be known for your cats all over this land. In the name of our village I will give you a purse of one hundred yen. This should take you to the Emperor's city of Kyoto where artists like you are honored."

202

That was the beginning of good luck for Yoda. With his one hundred yen he did go to Kyoto. People there paid him well to draw them pictures of cats.

The Emperor himself heard of the skill of this painter of cats. And he called Yoda to his palace. Yoda painted a famous cat screen for the Emperor. He painted other pictures as well, which were hung on the palace walls.

The young artist painted flowers and birds. He painted temples and mountain paths. But none of his pictures were so highly prized as his famous cats.

The Dog
That Learned
to Read

"A storyteller has come! A storyteller has come!" The news spread quickly one evening through a small village in India.

Men coming home from their day's work in the fields heard it. Children told their mothers. And everyone hurried to the great banyan tree in the village square.

The storyteller had sat down there to rest after his walk from the next village. In the cool of the evening, there he would tell them his tales. It would not cost much to listen, only a little rice and some of the melted butter, called ghee.

None of the people of this village had ever listened to a radio. None had ever heard of a moving picture or television play. For this was in the old times before such wonders were dreamed of.

A tale of a wandering storyteller was the best fun these

Indian people knew. With his quick changes of voice the storyteller became first one, then another, of the people in the tale. It was just like a play. One could hear a bird's feather drop, his listeners sat so still.

"In the name of Allah! Allah be with you!" the people greeted the storyteller on this evening in India.

"Allah give you peace!" the wandering teller-of-tales replied. "What story will you have first? A sad story? A story to make you glad? Or a story to make you laugh aloud? Which shall it be?"

"A tale to laugh at," the children cried.

"Yes, a tale for laughing," their fathers and mothers agreed.

The storyteller nodded his head in its high white turban. He settled himself more comfortably on the ground under the ancient tree. Then he told them this absurd tale of the dog that learned how to read.

In the country far away there once was a village. It was like all other villages. In it there were wise people and foolish ones, too. And the wisest, of course, was the Moolah, the teacher of the village school.

The best house in that village, as in most others, was the mosque, the House of the Great Allah and of Mohammed his Prophet. Here this Moolah lived. Here he had his school for the village boys.

"Our Moolah is the most learned man in all the world," the children of that village said. Everyone looked up to the

Moolah. Few people there could read or write in those times. So it was not strange that they admired those who could.

This village was in a part of India where the weather always was hot. It was better, the Moolah said, to have school out of doors, in the open square before the mosque.

There, under some trees, the boys sat around him. They held their books in their hands. They bent their heads over the pages. With loud voices they said over and over the words they had to learn. Many of these words they did not understand. But they only shouted them the louder.

Often visitors stopped at that school in the square. Men and women going along the highway stood and listened to the young pupils recite. Many shook their heads, wondering. For they themselves knew nothing of reading or books.

Such a one was the weaver of that Indian village. He could make very good cloth on his wood loom. But he could not read one word. Really, that weaver was not very smart. He was so stupid, indeed, that people often made fun of him.

One day while the weaver was watching, the Moolah was scolding one of his pupils.

"In the name of Allah," the Moolah cried, "you are the most stupid boy in this school. I teach you and teach you. I tell you this word and that word. But you do not trouble yourself to remember. I could teach a dog to read more easily than I can teach you."

The Moolah's patience must have been sorely tried. It

was not nice of him to compare that boy with a dog. For a dog was the lowest animal the Moolah could think of. In India, in those olden times, people said dogs were unclean. No one wanted to touch them.

Maybe that pupil did not pay much attention to the words of the Moolah. But the weaver, standing near, heard them. And the next day he came again to the school. This time he was leading his dog by a rope.

"I have brought my dog to your school, Moolah," the weaver said. "I want you to teach my dog how to read."

"I do not teach dogs," the Moolah replied in an angry voice. He thought the weaver was insulting him.

"Only yesterday, Learned Moolah, I heard you say you could easily teach a dog how to read. I heard you with my own ears.

"Now I have no children. Though he is but a dog, this animal is like a son to me. I want him taught how to read."

The Moolah laughed. "It is just that this weaver is so simple and so stupid," he thought. "He will never stop asking me to teach his dog to read. I will pretend to say yes."

"Well, then, Weaver," the Moolah said, "I will take your dog into my school. But like any other pupil, his learning will have to be paid for."

"Have no fear for your pay, Moolah! I gladly will pay. Teach my dog how to read, and I will bring you cloth enough for a robe and a turban as well." The weaver went away happy, leaving his dog behind with the Moolah.

Some days later the weaver stopped at the school to ask about the new pupil.

"Allah give you peace, Moolah," the weaver said. "Does my dog know his letters?"

"You shall see, Weaver," the Moolah was ready for him. "You shall even watch your dog read. But you must stand over here, well out of his way. He must not turn and see you."

The clever Moolah laid a big book down before the dog. Between the pages of this book, he had put a few bits of dry meat. The dog sniffed the good smell. He kept his nose down near the book. Now and again when he had eaten one bit of meat, the dog pawed at the pages of the book to get the next bit.

"He truly is reading," the simple weaver called out in his joy. "I can see his mouth move as he forms the words. I can see him turn the pages. Truly, O Moolah, in all this broad land there is no teacher like you!"

And he went away happy, leaving his dog to finish his schooling there at the mosque.

It may be that the dog did not care for school. Or it may be he followed some stranger out of the village. For that very night he gnawed through his rope, and ran away from the Moolah.

What should the teacher say when the weaver came back to get his dog? Well, any story would do. The silly weaver would believe whatever tale he was told.

"Has my dog learned to read all the way through the

book?" the weaver asked when he came back at last. And the Moolah replied,

"Oh yes, your dog has learned to read many books. He is so learned that he has turned into a judge. He is now a wise Cadi and he wears a Cadi's turban.

"Indeed, Weaver," the Moolah went on, trying not to laugh, "your dog is so wise that they have made him the Cadi of our part of the country."

No doubt the Moolah thought the weaver would know right away that this was a joke. He only mentioned the Cadi of that part of the country because he did not like the real one. He disliked the judge so much that he often secretly spoke of him as "that dog of a Cadi."

But the simple weaver thought it was no more wonderful for a dog to become a Cadi than for a dog to learn to read. He gave the Moolah the cloth for his new robe and new turban. And next day he set out for the town where the Cadi was holding court.

He carried with him a bag of juicy goat bones. For that was the food his dog liked the best. And he went to the Cadi's court.

"Goat bones for you, my faithful friend!" the stupid weaver cried when he stood there before the court. He waved the strong-smelling bag under the nose of the Cadi.

"Here's a good dinner for you. Come and eat!" the weaver called, just as he would have called to his dog.

"The man surely is crazy," the Cadi said to those near

him. "We must treat him with care in front of all these people in the court."

The Cadi rose from his judge's seat. "We shall now take a short rest," he told the people. And he led the weaver to one side where no one could overhear what was said.

"Who are you? What do you want with me?" the Cadi asked.

"Do you not know me? I am your master," the weaver cried out. "You were my dog who watched over my house. Do you not remember how I paid the Moolah to teach you to read? I saw you at your reading with my own eyes.

"No dog should forget his master, even though he has gone to school. Just because you have turned into a Cadi is no reason to be so ungrateful."

"This man is completely crazy." The Cadi shook his head sadly. "It will be best for me to humor him. Then he will go away." And he said to the weaver,

"In becoming a Cadi, I no doubt forgot my past. It may well be true that I once was your dog. But do not tell it here. Or these people will not want me for their judge.

"Truly, I am not ungrateful," the Cadi said softly. "Here is my purse. In it you will find one hundred rupees. Surely that is enough to buy freedom for any dog, even a dog that knows how to read. Take the purse! Go, and Allah give you peace!"

"Oh, I will keep your secret, Wise Cadi." The simple weaver nodded his head knowingly. "I will tell no one that

211

once you were my dog. And I will never trouble you here again."

Everyone was happy. The Moolah was happy with his new robe and his new turban. The weaver was happy with his hundred rupees. And the Cadi thought it well worth the money to get the crazy man out of his court.

No doubt the dog, also, was happy. No doubt he found a wiser master. For there could not have been any other as stupid as that weaver was.

The Old Dog and the Gray Wolf

In the old, old days in Russia, there once lived a man whose name was Ivan. His log house stood on the edge of a village of other log houses like his. And each day Ivan went out with other men to work in the fields of the rich lord of the land.

Ivan was not rich himself. But he lived happily enough in his little log house. He and his family had no great treasures, it is true. But they had a good dog to guard those things they did own.

Ivan's dog once had been a fine watchdog. When he was younger, the dog had barked fiercely. He had let no one come near the little log house.

Now the trouble was that Ivan's dog was growing old.

Sometimes, in his sleep, the old dog did not hear footsteps. He almost never barked now at the right time. His master was tired of giving good food to a dog who did not do his work.

"Our old dog is no good, Wife," Ivan said one day at last. "I shall just take him out into the woods and hang him from a tree."

"Oh, no! No! Do not do that, I pray you," the good woman begged her husband. "Our dog has served us well. All his life he has watched over our house. Surely you will not kill him now, just because he is old. Send the dog away, if you must. But do not hang him from a tree."

Ivan shook his head. It would be far better to end the dog's life there and then.

He put a strong rope about the neck of the old dog. And he led him into the deep woods. The man was about to throw the other end of the rope over a branch of a tree, when he saw his dog was crying. Great tears were rolling down the dog's nose.

"Well then, Old Dog, I will not hang you." The man's hard heart had melted at the sight of his dog crying so sadly.

"But he who does not work should not eat," the man said to the dog. "You cannot live in my house and eat my food any longer. I will tie you here to this tree, that you may not follow me home. The good God shall decide whether you live or you die."

Whining and sad, the old dog lay down under the tree. Tears still rolled down his face as he thought of his unhappy fate. He was still crying and crying, when a large gray wolf passed by.

Now, in those days, people say, wolves were not nearly so fierce as they are in our times. This large gray wolf looked friendly enough. His great open mouth almost seemed to be smiling as he spoke to the dog.

"Why do you cry so, Old Dog?" asked the gray wolf.

"It is that I am too old to guard my master's house any more," the dog told the wolf. "If I do not do my work, then I may not eat. My master has put me out of his house. The good God will decide whether I live or I die.

"I expect I shall die," the old dog went on sadly. "How shall I eat? I am too old to catch rabbits. And I never was a very good catcher-of-rabbits even when I was young."

"Ay, the rabbits run fast," the gray wolf agreed. "And old legs are slow. There is only one thing to do. You must make your master take you back into his house. We must think of a plan."

There in the forest, the old dog and the gray wolf sat thinking and thinking. Then the wolf cried, "I have it. I have a plan, Old Dog. Whom does your master love most in the world?"

"That is easy to answer, Gray Wolf," the old dog replied. "My master loves most his dear little granddaughter, Marya. My master loves that tiny girl more than his wife, more than his own daughter."

"Then it must be Marya who helps you get back into your home. What if you should save the life of the small

215

Marya? Would Ivan not take you back into his house then? Listen, Old Dog, here is how it can be done.

"Tomorrow as always," the gray wolf explained, "the child will go with her mother to take dinner to the men out in the fields. When the woman is not looking, I will creep out of the woods. I will snatch up the child and pretend to run off with her.

"Oh, I will do it gently. I will do Marya no harm. But you shall attack me. You shall pretend to make my fur fly. I will act frightened. I will let the child go and run fast away."

The old dog was greatly pleased with this plan. It was a fine plan, he thought, and one that might work. Surely his master would reward him if he saved Marya from a wolf. Surely soon he would be lying again in his warm place by the stove in the log house.

The gray wolf gnawed through the rope that tied the old dog to the tree. And together the two plotters went off to make their plans for the next day.

All went well. As always, Ivan's daughter and his beloved grandchild, Marya, set out from the log house just at noon. In their hands they carried baskets of food for the hungry men out in the fields.

Under a shady tree on the edge of the fields, the baskets were set down. Little Marya waited beside them while her mother went off to call the men to their dinner.

The men put down their hoes and their scythes. They started across the fields toward their dinner baskets. Then, to their horror, they saw a gray wolf creep out of the forest and grab up the child.

With a great cry, Ivan started to run. He ran very fast, but his faithful old dog reached the child first. Barking and snarling, the dog attacked the wolf. The fur seemed to fly, and the wolf ran away. When Ivan came up, the old dog was licking the face and the hands of the little girl.

It all happened so quickly that little Marya had not had time to make even one cry. So gently had the gray wolf picked her up that she had not even one scratch.

Oh yes, the plan of the gray wolf and the old dog was a great success. The child's mother put her arms around the old dog's shaggy neck. Ivan himself patted the old dog on the head.

"From now on, nothing is too good for our old dog," Ivan said to his wife that night. "So long as he lives, he shall have his warm place by our stove. Whether he barks or not, he shall have all the food he can eat."

The old dog was happy then. Down in his heart, of course, he felt a little bit badly about the trick he had played on his master. Though he never said so, the dog was not now so glad to meet the gray wolf on the road. Often he ran away before the wolf saw him coming.

One day, however, he came face to face with the gray wolf. There was no chance to slink out of sight under a bush.

"Good day, Old Dog," the gray wolf said. "I hear there is to be a wedding at your house next week."

"Yes, there will be a wedding. My master's youngest daughter is to be married. But what has our wedding to do with you, Gray Wolf?"

"It is only that people say there will be a fine feast. There will be good things to eat, and vodka to drink. I have never been to a wedding. I should like to come to this one." The gray wolf spoke as if he was sure the old dog would say yes.

"That never could be," the old dog shook his head. "My master would never invite a wolf to our wedding."

"Then you could invite me," the gray wolf said with a sly smile. "You could open the door for me. You could hide me away where no one would see me."

"That I will not do," the old dog growled at the thought. "It would lose me my warm place by the stove if I brought you to our wedding."

"And," said the wolf softly, "it will lose you your warm place by the stove if you do not. Suppose Ivan should learn what really happened to Marya that day out in the fields! It would be too bad if someone told him how he had been tricked."

The old dog hung his head. He knew the gray wolf was clever. He just might find some way to tell Ivan the true story.

"Very well, Gray Wolf," the old dog gave in at last. "I do not like it, but you shall come to the wedding. You shall creep into the house. I will open the door. And you shall come in while all the people are away at the church. I will

218

hide you up on the stove. But you will have to keep very still there."

The brick stove in Ivan's log house was not very high. A wood bench stood near it. It was no trouble at all for the wolf to jump up on its flat top.

A gentle warmth came up through the bricks of the stove. The wolf curled himself up there on its top to wait until the wedding feast should begin.

The merry wedding party came back into the log house. They ate and they drank. Nobody noticed that the old dog carried pieces of juicy meat and bits of black bread to his friend on the top of the stove.

"I am thirsty, Old Dog," the gray wolf said after a while. "I have eaten all I can hold. Now I want something to drink. Bring me a bottle of vodka, like that which the real guests are drinking."

Don't ask me how the dog managed to get hold of a bottle of vodka. Don't ask me how he got it up on top of the stove. The story says that he did and that the wolf drank the vodka down as if it were just water.

Everyone knows what a bad drink vodka is. How it sets one's head turning and turning. How it makes one feel like dancing. And how in the end it is sure to make one very drunk.

That is what happened to the gray wolf. When he had emptied the bottle down his throat, he gave a great howl. He howled and he howled, although he declared he was singing. He danced and he danced there on top of the stove.

219

At last he danced himself right over the edge. With a howl he fell flat upon the kitchen floor.

"A wolf is in the kitchen! A gray wolf is there!" the girls screamed. The men shouted and ran to get sticks to drive the gray wolf away.

The old dog barked his loudest. He pretended to snap at the wolf.

"Run, Wolf, run!" the dog whispered. "Or they will beat you to death."

Somehow or other the gray wolf managed to get out of the door. His poor legs were shaking. His head was spinning. But he got away safe into the forest, with the dog running after him.

Everyone said it was the old dog that had chased the wolf away from the log house. Once again the old dog was the hero of the day.

After that the old dog took care to keep out of the way of the wolf. He knew that the angry wolf would be looking for him. He was sure that the wolf would like to tear him to pieces. But how was it his fault? It was the gray wolf who behaved badly, not the old dog.

Some people say this story explains why the wolf and the dog are no longer friendly. I do not know if this is so. But I do know that no dog is safe now if a wolf is nearby.

The Enchanted
Black Cat

This story may remind you of a tale you already know, the tale of Cinderella. In this one, too, there is a good, pretty maiden who had an unkind stepmother and a cross, ugly stepsister. There is a pair of tiny slippers as well. But instead of a fairy godmother there is only a big black cat.

The pretty girl's name was Marie. She was the daughter of an ancient French nobleman. And she lived with her father in a castle on the shore of a large lake.

Marie's own mother had died. Her father had married again. The nobleman thought his new wife would be a loving stepmother for his dear daughter. He thought the woman's own child, Louise, would be her kind sister.

But Marie's stepmother was not kind and loving as most stepmothers are. She hated the girl because she was so much prettier than her own cross-faced Louise.

Because of her gentle ways, Marie was beloved by all in the castle. No one liked Louise there because she had such

222

a bad temper. No one liked the stepmother either, because she was so unkind to their beloved Marie.

It was Louise who wore the fine clothes and shining jewels. It was Louise who had the best food. It was Louise who rode out in the nobleman's carriage. Marie stayed at home with only her big black cat to keep her company in her tower room.

One day the castle was filled with excitement. The Prince of that part of the land was on his way there. He was seeking a bride, so it was told. You see, the fame of Marie's beauty and goodness was spread all over France. If she was as pretty and good as everyone said, the Prince would make her his wife.

But the stepmother wanted the Prince for her own daughter. She meant, by good deed or by bad deed, to see that it was her Louise whom the Prince should wed.

For help the nobleman's wife went to her best friend, who was a witch. A clever witch this friend was, no doubt the cleverest witch in all the land.

"When the Prince comes, it must be the pretty Marie whom he shall meet," this witch advised. "But on the wedding day, it will be Louise who is under the bride's veil." This was the trick which the two planned to play on the Prince.

"But take care, my friend!" the witch said at the last. "Take care that a black cat does not cross your daughter's path."

No doubt the stepmother forgot this last warning in her

plans for the Prince's coming. She dressed Marie up in Louise's silk gown. She put Louise's jewels upon her. But neither the silk gown nor the jewels were half so bright and shining as the sweet face of the girl herself.

"I bring golden slippers for my bride to wear at our wedding," the good Prince said to Marie. Her beauty and goodness had won his heart at first sight. With his own hands he fitted the tiny golden shoes upon Marie's little feet. And the wedding day was set for the very next week.

But on that great day, poor Marie sat alone in her tower room. Not even her black cat had stayed behind with her. All were at the church to see the Prince take his bride.

That day, just as the witch had said, it was Louise who was wearing the fine wedding dress. It was Louise's cross, ugly face that was hidden under the bride's veil. And it was Louise's big feet that were squeezed into the Prince's slippers of gold.

How Louise's feet hurt! Marie had walked about in the golden slippers with comfort and ease. But Louise could get only two of her toes into each little shoe. The nobleman's servants had to carry the girl out to her coach.

Of course, the Prince thought the girl under the wedding veil was the bride he had chosen. In the shine of the satin gown, and the glitter of the jewels, he could not see very well the face under the veil.

But when they came to the church the Prince quickly saw that something was wrong. For the bride could not walk alone from her coach to the church door. At each step she gave a cry as if she were in pain. Her maids held her from falling. And the Prince ran to see what was the matter.

Now the cruel stepmother, indeed, forgot what her friend, the witch, had said about a black cat. When she locked Marie up in her tower room, she did not make sure the girl's black cat was there with her.

The woman was greatly surprised to see the animal jump down out of the wedding coach. And she was afraid when the black cat ran to the Prince, miaouing and miaouing.

"Can it be that this cat speaks?" the Prince cried aloud. "I thought I heard the cat say these very words:

"The Ugly One! The Ugly One!
  She's giving you the Ugly One!

"The Pretty One! The Pretty One!
  In the tower waits for you to come!"

Before the stepmother could stop him, the Prince lifted the bride's veil. And when he saw the cross, ugly face of Louise, he cried out, "This black cat speaks truly. A trick has been played here. This is not the bride I have chosen. And I will wed no other than my dear Marie. When Marie is made ready, I will come back."

The Prince mounted his horse and he galloped away to his palace on the other side of the lake.

They say it was the witch also who told the cruel stepmother what she should do next.

"So long as the fair Marie dwells in this castle, the Prince

225

will never marry your daughter. Get rid of the girl!" This was the wicked advice which the witch gave her friend.

That very night, when the nobleman was asleep, the stepmother led Marie down to the edge of the lake. The wind was high and the lake waters were rough.

"You are going on a journey, my girl," the woman said. "Hurry, now! Hurry! There is but little time."

"May I not say good-by to my dear father," Marie was weeping now.

"There is no time." Her stepmother pushed the girl into the sailboat.

"May I not take my black cat along with me for company?"

"You can take that cat and welcome!" The stepmother was glad enough to get rid of the beast which had betrayed her to the Prince.

So the black cat was put into the sailboat with Marie. And while the moon still shone in the sky, the two of them were pushed far out from shore in the little boat.

Next morning the nobleman missed his dear daughter. But by that time the sail had carried Marie's boat far across the broad lake. No one from the castle could find her.

The wind blew the sailboat hither and thither over the lake. At last it blew Marie and her cat up on the shore of a small island.

No other living thing did they find there. There was no one to tell them that the palace they saw, nearby on the mainland, was the home of Marie's Prince.

226

For some days Marie and the black cat lived in a cave on that little island. When the food they had brought with them was gone, Marie gathered berries and fruit. The cat scooped some tiny fish out of the lake. But truly they did not have much to eat.

"I must go to the mainland to get us some food," the black cat said to Marie. "I will ride over the lake on this log of wood."

The cat would not hear of Marie's going with him. She was safer, he said, in their island cave.

"Make me a big bag to carry on my back," the cat said to the girl. "I will go to the palace yonder. And I will bring back good food."

Marie watched her dear black cat jump on the log. And she saw the log float him safely across to the mainland.

Once the black cat was on land, he threw his big bag over his shoulder. And he set out for the palace. He made a strange sight as he went along the city street. For he walked upright, on his hind legs, just like a man.

The palace gates were wide open. The cat marched straight through them and into the kitchen where the Prince's dinner was cooking.

"Scat! Scat!" the cook cried. "Go away, Cat!" and she started after the cat with her broom.

"Wait a bit, Mother! Is your master at home?" The cat spoke to the cook in the words of men. This so frightened the woman that her broom fell from her hand.

"My master has not yet come home for his dinner, but

228

he soon will be here." Somehow the surprised cook managed to answer the cat.

"Well, I cannot wait for him," that bold cat replied. "I will just take this roast chicken and this piece of fried bacon. My dear sister is hungry. I must bring her food quickly."

"You cannot take the good dinner I have cooked for the Prince," the cook cried in a rage. "No, you cannot have it."

"I must have it, woman," the black cat said fiercely. "I must have also a loaf of fresh bread and a bottle of wine."

Now, before the cook could think what to say or to do, the cat had put the chicken, the bacon, the bread, and the wine into his bag. And he was gone.

That day, Marie and her black cat ate well on their little island. But the Prince had to content himself with a very poor meal.

"Oh, my dear master," the cook tried to excuse the food she set out for the Prince, "I had cooked you a chicken and a good piece of bacon. And a strange black cat walked right into my kitchen. On his hind legs he walked, just like a man. That cat must know magic, for he talked like a man, too.

"The cat grabbed up your dinner. I lifted my broom to stop him. But by his magic, my broom dropped from my hand. And the cat was gone."

"How can you expect me to believe such a story?" The Prince was hungry and cross.

"You shall see it for yourself, Master," the cook was

almost weeping. "That magic black cat said he was coming back here tomorrow to get some more food."

Next day the Prince was there waiting. He had his gun in his hand when the cat came.

"Surely I have seen this black cat before," the Prince said to himself.

"Ho, Cat, where have I seen you?" he cried aloud. And his gun dropped to his side while he waited for the cat's answer.

"Do you not remember, good Prince?" Words did indeed come out of the cat's mouth. "It was on the steps of the church, on your wedding day. It was I who warned you of the wicked trick they were playing upon you. Remember how I said:

"The Ugly One! The Ugly One!
  She's giving you the Ugly One!

"The Pretty One! The Pretty One!
  In the tower waits for you to come."

The Prince knew then that this was the black cat who had saved him from marrying the wrong bride.

"Where is the Pretty One now, Cat?" the Prince asked eagerly. And when the cat told his story, the young man lost no time in going to look for Marie.

With the cat by his side, the Prince sailed in a fine boat to the little island. Marie welcomed him with a glad smile. Even without her silken robes and her bright jewels, the girl seemed to the Prince the fairest in all the world.

The wedding of Marie and the Prince took place at his palace the very next day. Everyone came, the rich and the poor. And everyone marveled at the beauty and sweetness of the Prince's bride. They marveled, too, that a black cat should have his own seat at the banquet. No one told them at that time why the black cat was so honored.

Oh, Marie was happy with her good Prince. But still she could not help thinking of her father who loved her so much.

"If only I could see my dear father once more," Marie said to the Prince. "I should like him to know that I am your bride."

The Prince had four horses put to his royal coach. And he rode with his bride in splendid style to the home of her father. The black cat went along with them, sitting beside the driver, just like a footman.

How happy was the father when he saw his dear Marie once again! And how enraged was her stepmother!

But the woman hid her anger. She welcomed the guests with a fine feast, to which she asked all the neighbors. Her friend the witch was there. No doubt the two of them still were making plots.

When everybody was seated, Marie's big black cat walked into the room. He jumped up on the table, just at the place where the wicked witch sat. The black cat's eyes blazed like the lightning. He humped up his back, and he began to spit into the witch's face.

"Take away that black cat," the stepmother cried. And the witch's face turned as white as the tablecloth.

"Wait! Wait!" the cat spoke aloud, while everyone wondered.

"This woman is a witch," the cat said. "She and her friend here are the ones who tried to do away with our dear Marie.

"Woman," the cat turned to face the witch, "now your last hour is near."

"I am not afraid of you, Black Cat," the witch screamed her answer. "I will fight if you touch me. I will fight you with water. I will fight you with wind. I will fight you with fire. We shall see then whose magic is strongest."

This battle would be something to see, the banquet guests thought. They crowded onto the balcony as the witch and the cat ran down into the courtyard.

"First fight me with water," the black cat called to the witch.

They began to spit at each other, the witch and the cat. But for one barrel of water which the witch spit at the cat, the cat spit three barrels. And the witch was the first one to cry "Stop."

"Now I shall fight you with wind!" It was the witch's turn to choose.

The two began to blow at each other. Great blasts of wind came from their mouths. They blew with all their might. But the wind blown by the witch was only a breeze compared with the wind blown up by the cat.

A stormy blast came out of the cat's mouth. It blew the witch about, just as if she were a leaf. To the right, to the left, against the palace walls, she was thrown. Soon she cried out for mercy.

"Only fire is left now," the cat cried. He opened his mouth and great flames came forth. The witch breathed fire, too. Like dragons, they fought. But for one blast of fire from the witch, there were three from the cat. In no time at all the witch was burned up. All that was left of her was a small heap of ashes.

Then the cat turned toward Marie's cruel stepmother.

"Sister of a witch, now it is your turn." And in a moment that wicked woman was gone, too. Only a few ashes were left in her place.

"How can we thank you, good friend?" the Prince then said to the cat. "What can we do for you in return for the magic deeds you have done for us this day?"

"You can lay your sharp sword upon the skin of my back. You can slit it in two, O Prince," the cat answered.

"But we would not hurt you like that, my dear cat." It was Marie who spoke then.

"Do as I ask you, Prince," the cat said. And as everyone watched, the cat's skin was slit. Lo, from it there rose a tall handsome man.

"It was that very witch who put her spell upon me when I was not watching," the tall man explained. "It was only when I had killed this witch that I could be free from my cat's skin."

233

All the banquet guests drank to the Prince and Marie. They drank to the stranger, and they drank to the nobleman. They even drank to poor ugly Louise when Marie asked them to do so. And everyone hoped, now that her wicked mother was gone, this bad-tempered girl would learn to be more like her good stepsister.

The Wild Dog and the King's Son

In the long-ago times when animals talked and dogs were still wild, there was a certain king in the part of Europe now known as Yugoslavia. In those early times, kings, like other men, spent their days hunting out in the forest.

One day this King, hunting for deer, saw a brown shape move amid the trees. He threw his spear at it, and a howl came out of the bushes. He had hit a wild dog.

That wild dog was like no other animal that King ever had seen. He ordered his men to tie it up well and take it back to the castle.

"Put the beast in a strong cage where I can watch it," the King gave the order.

235

Everyone in the castle came to look at the wild dog. But the one who came most often was the King's son, Mihail.

Other beasts had been put into that cage before. But no animal in it had ever cried so loud and so long as this wild dog. Prince Mihail's good heart was touched.

"Let the beast go free, my father," Prince Mihail begged. "You would not eat the meat of a wolf-creature like this. Let it go free."

"This one is not a wolf," the King replied. "I shall decide whether to eat it or not, later on. But I will not let it go free. If anyone dares to open its cage, he shall be put to death."

Well, one day followed another. Still the wild dog did not stop crying. One night when the moon was full, the dog howled more sadly than ever before.

Mihail could not sleep. He could not forget the dog in the cage. He knew it was wrong, but he crept out of the castle. And he set the dog free.

With one joyous yelp, the wild dog was gone into the woods. And next morning no sound came from the empty cage.

"Who has set my beast free? Let me but find him and he shall be put to death!" Oh, the King was in a great rage.

Now the King's son, Mihail, for all he had a soft heart, was not a coward.

"It was I, Father." Mihail stepped forth from the crowd

around the empty cage. "I could not stand to hear the poor beast cry. I set him free."

Then the King wished he had not spoken so quickly. He loved his son truly. He did not want him to die. Yet he could not take back his words.

The courtiers, too, loved Prince Mihail. Now they knelt at the King's feet, and they cried, "Mercy, Your Majesty! Mercy for Prince Mihail! Send him away if he must be punished. But do not put him to death."

"So shall it be!" the King said then. In his heart he was glad his son would not have to die.

"Mihail shall go far, far away. And he shall not come back here for a year and a day."

The Young Prince made ready for his sad journey. He packed up his fine clothes. He saddled his horse. He was ready to start.

"You are young and foolish, my son," the King said to Mihail. "You will need someone to look after you. Our servant, Petar, shall go with you into the wide world. Petar shall walk by your horse's side. And he shall carry, always within reach, this letter about you.

"The letter tells other kings that you are a king's son. It will make sure of your welcome into their kingdoms."

Mihail and the servant, Petar, set forth into the wide world. They went on and on, finding shelter and food wherever they could.

One day when the noonday sun shone hot upon them, they grew very thirsty.

237

"Ah, here is a well, Master," the servant, Petar, said at last. "But there is no pail with which we can dip out the water. There is no cup either."

Mihail jumped down and tied his horse to a tree. Then he looked into the well.

"The water is not very far from the top of the well," he said to the servant. "You shall hold me tight by my feet, Petar. Then I can reach the water with my lips."

Upside down, head below heels, the young man did drink. The servant Petar held him tight by his feet until he had finished.

"Now draw me up again, and take your turn," the upside-down young Prince called to the servant. But to his surprise, the servant made no move to pull him out of the well.

"I shall not pull you out of this well, my young master, unless you promise to change places with me," that bold fellow said. "I must put on your clothes. I must ride on your horse. I must know what it is like to be a king's son. Swear before Heaven to do what I ask. Or I will drop you down, down, and down into this deep well."

What could Mihail do? His servant had only to let go of his feet, and he would drown. No, there was nothing else for the young Prince to do but to give his word. And the man, Petar, knew that once this word had been given, the Prince would not go back on it.

So Petar, the servant, dressed himself in the clothes of Mihail, the Prince. He took Mihail's place in the saddle. It

238

was Prince Mihail who walked now, while Petar rode on the horse.

It was thus that they came into the neighboring land. Petar, the servant, lost no time in sending into the castle the King's letter saying he was the son of a king.

"Welcome, son of a king. A welcome guest you are here!" This was the greeting they gave to the servant in his princely clothes.

"And you, fellow, take your master's horse to the stable. You can make yourself a bed near it, on the straw there." This was the greeting they gave the true prince in the servant's dress.

They made feasts for the false prince. They held hunting parties in his honor. Oh, Petar had a fine time, pretending to be the King's son.

Still the man never was quite easy in his own mind.

"Suppose Prince Mihail one day grows tired of his bargain," Petar said to himself. "Suppose one day he tells the King that I am his servant and he is the Prince? I am not safe yet. I must think of some plan to get that young prince forever out of my way."

It must have been the custom in those times for kings to keep wild animals in their castle gardens. This King, like Mihail's father, had his own private zoo. It was seeing the wild beasts there that gave Petar his wicked idea.

"You have many beasts, Majesty," Petar said to the King. "What huge bears! What fierce wolves! It must cost a great deal to feed so many beasts. Why do you not send them out into the woods to get their food for themselves? A servant could go with them. He could bring them home at the sunset."

"But how could any man get all my beasts home again? And would not the beasts kill him?" The King was surprised at Petar's suggestion.

"Oh, my own servant could easily do it, Your Majesty," Petar said. "The fellow is very fond of wild beasts. And I'll gladly lend him for the task. If he should be killed, it would be no great matter."

So the next morning the King sent for Mihail.

"Your master tells me you have a love for wild animals, fellow," the King said to Mihail. "He says you would gladly drive my beasts to the forest to find their own food. He declares you can bring them safely back home. You shall begin with the bears, and woe be unto you if every one of them is not back in his cage when the sun sets!"

Nothing poor Mihail could say would change the King's order. The bears' cages were opened, and the great beasts ran off into the woods.

Mihail ran after them. He looked for them all through the forest. But he could not find even one bear.

The poor young man sat down upon a big stone. His heart was heavy. He felt almost like weeping.

"The king surely will have me killed if I do not bring back his bears. What, what shall I do?" Mihail cried aloud.

Just then he felt something cold touch his hand. He looked down and saw that it was the cold nose of a beast.

Wonder of wonders! It was the very wild dog he had set free in his father's garden.

How had the wild dog come so far? Mihail never found out. But there the beast was, at his side.

"Do not look so sad, my friend," the wild dog said to the King's son. "Take this little bell that hangs round my neck. Ring it when you are in trouble. And help will come to you."

"Will the bell help me to take the King's bears back to their cages?" Mihail was thinking that already he was in trouble.

"Ring the bell and see, Mihail," the wild dog said. Then he was gone.

When the sun was near setting, Mihail rang the dog's bell. He wished out loud that it would help him to lead the bears home.

There were shouts from the courtiers when they saw the young man returning. They called the King to come quickly and see the strange sight.

In front of Mihail, just like tame bears in a circus, all the King's bears were dancing. Mihail was playing a gay little tune upon a small flute. And the huge bears danced themselves right into their pens.

Next day, Mihail was ordered to take the King's wolves out into the forest. As before, the wild beasts at once dashed away out of his sight.

As on the day before, too, Mihail rang the bell which the wild dog had given him. Again, at the castle, all were struck dumb with wonder. At the sunset the fierce wolves came home again. They ran at Mihail's side like so many tame dogs.

"Surely Prince Mihail could never bring back the King's doves. Surely he could not gather wild birds out of the sky." Petar thought this would be one task which his master could not do. So he persuaded the King to give this order next.

The wild doves flew free, up, up toward the sun. Higher and higher they soared, until they were lost in the clouds.

Mihail, sitting upon the big stone, began once more to weep.

"Never, oh never, will I be able to bring the King's doves back again." The young man spoke aloud. And again he felt the touch of the cold nose of the wild dog on his hand.

"Where is your faith, my friend?" the animal said. "Ring my bell! And believe in me! All will be well."

So when the sun was low in the western sky, the sound of the bell rose into the air. At once the wild doves began dropping like rain, out of the clouds. They sat on the Prince's shoulders. They lit on his outstretched arms. They even perched on his head.

"Never was there another young man like this one," the courtiers said to the King. "What evil luck can have brought so noble and fearless a youth to be a servant?"

"Who are you, fellow, that you can charm the beasts and the birds?" the King asked Mihail that night.

"I will tell you, O King," Mihail replied. "I will tell of

243

the bargain I had to make with my wicked servant. For it is a servant in my own princely clothes whom you treat as my father's son. It is I who am Mihail, the King's son. It is he who is Petar, the servant, sent to attend me."

All in that King's court marveled at the tale of the wild dog and the King's son. They stripped the fine clothes off of Petar. And they threw him into a dungeon for the trick he had played on their King.

Now the tables were turned. Now it was Mihail who sat at the King's side at the royal feasts. Now it was the true Prince who rode with the King forth to the hunt. And it was with Prince Mihail that the King's daughter fell deeply in love.

You can guess how it all ended. How this King gladly gave his daughter in marriage to the brave young Prince who could tame the beasts and the birds.

Everyone was happy, but especially the bears, the wolves, and the doves. For a wedding gift, the young bridegroom asked only that the wild creatures should be set free. His request was gladly granted. The bride's father, the King, was a little ashamed of the part he had played in Petar's wicked plot.

The story does not tell what became of the wild dog. It may be the animal came to live with his friend Mihail. If he did, I am sure he soon forgot his wild ways and became a true dog.

"General" Dog
and His Army

Once upon a time—perhaps a thousand or two years ago—
there lived in Yugoslavia a certain young man. His name
was Branko, and his family once had been rich.

But bad luck found its way into the young Branko's
castle. His father and mother came to the end of their days.
His servants all fell ill, or they went away. Somehow there
was no longer so much money to spend.

At last the young man was left all alone in his ancient
castle. His only treasures were his gun, and his horse, and
his faithful dog.

It would be hard to say which of these three treasures
Branko loved the most. His horse carried him forth to his
hunting each day. His gun brought down the wild animals
he needed for food. But his dog was his beloved friend and

companion. His dog guarded his castle at night. His dog never left his side during the day. Oh, it was his dog that Branko loved best.

One day Branko was riding through the thick forest, and his dog was running along by his horse's side. Suddenly the dog disappeared into the bushes, barking and barking. Branko jumped from his saddle. He tied the horse to a tree and followed the dog. Surely there must be some wild animal near.

While the man and the dog were out of sight, a fox came along to where the horse was tied to the tree.

"A fine horse is this one. Well fed, and well cared for!" The fox spoke aloud. "You must have a good master, Horse. I will just keep you company until your master comes back."

Branko was surprised to see a fox sitting there by his horse. He dropped the young deer he had been carrying, and he raised his gun to shoot. But the fox spoke in time.

"Don't shoot me, Master! I am seeking a home. Let me be your servant and live in your castle! Let me care for your horse! Let me keep watch in your stable."

The fox begged so hard that Branko at last agreed. He truly needed a stableboy.

"We will try it," he said to the fox. "But you will have to serve me well. And you will have to take orders from my dog. My dog has charge of my castle and everything in it."

Next day when Branko, his horse, and his dog went out

to hunt, the fox went along with them. While Branko followed his dog into the bushes, the fox stayed behind to
watch out for the horse.

It was well that he did, for while Branko was gone, a bear
came along.

"Don't you dare touch this horse, Bear," the fox cried
before the beast could come too near. "It belongs to my
master. And what a good master he is! It is warm in my
master's house. There is plenty to eat. Why do you not
come into his service, too?"

"Perhaps I will," the bear answered. He lay down nearby
to wait until Branko should come back.

It was strange to see a bear and a fox and a horse, all three
close together. Branko lifted his gun to shoot at the bear,
but the fox stopped him, crying,

"Do not shoot the bear, Master. He is a friend. He also
wishes to serve you and live in your castle."

"Good," Branko said. "I need a strong servant. But you
can only live in my castle, Bear, if you serve me well. You
must take orders, too, from my dear dog. He has charge of
my house."

Other animals heard what a good master Branko was.
One day it was a wolf who wanted to be his servant. Another day it was a mouse. Then a mole and a hare asked if
they, too, could live in the castle of this young man.

Strangest of all Branko's strange servants was a giant
bird, which was called a kumrekusha. The kumrekusha was
so big that she could lift a horse right up into the air. The

great bird was so strong that Branko himself could ride on her back up into the clouds.

Branko was kind to his animal servants. He fed them all well. He never worked them too hard. They loved their good master dearly. And they all seemed quite willing to take orders from Branko's dog.

One day the dog called the household together.

"We have the best master in all the world. Is that not true?" the dog asked the fox and the bear, the wolf and the mouse, the mole and the hare, and the big kumrekusha.

"Aye! Aye! True! True!" Shouts came from them all.

"There is nothing we would not do for our good master," the dog said then.

"Aye! Aye! True! True!" the animals shouted again.

"Well, our master is lonely. He needs a wife. We must find him a bride. She must be a young bride and a fair bride. None but the fairest bride in all this land will do for our master."

"But the fairest bride in this land is the daughter of the King," the little mouse cried. The animals nodded their heads. The mouse ought to know. She could get inside of any house. She had seen all the fair maids in all the land.

"How shall we ever bring the King's daughter here to our master's castle?" The animals shook their heads. They knew that the King kept his daughter shut up in a tall tower inside a walled garden.

"The kumrekusha can do it. And I will help her." The clever fox thought of a plan right away.

"I will ride on the back of the kumrekusha. She shall drop me down into the King's garden, and there I will change myself into a kitten. When the Princess comes out to play with me, the kumrekusha can easily carry her off."

This was a bold plan. But it was worth the trying, so the animals thought.

The kumrekusha dropped the fox inside the walls of the garden. And straightway the fox turned himself into a kitten, a little kitten as snowy white as the clouds.

From her tower window the Princess saw the little white cat. She watched it play with a butterfly, then hide under a rosebush. And she ran down into the garden to lift the pussy cat up into her arms.

Just as she did so, the giant bird caught the Princess gently up in her claws. She flew straight away with her to Branko's castle.

How surprised Branko was to see the fair bride which his animals had found for him! How gladly he asked the Princess to be his wife! How gladly, also, the King's daughter consented to marry this handsome young man!

Quickly the plans were made and the wedding took place. Happily the Princess took up her new life in the castle of Branko. The animals all served her well, as well as they served their dear master, Branko.

But the father of the fair bride was not at all happy. The King flew into a rage when he heard his dear daughter had been carried away by the tricks of a cat and a bird.

Where the Princess had gone, no one could tell the King. He offered a rich reward for any news of her. And a gypsy came to the palace.

"I have news of the Princess," the gypsy said. "She now is the bride of a noble young man, Branko by name. She dwells, happy and gay, in Branko's old castle, where all the servants are animals. Among them are the cat (truly a fox) and the giant bird, the kumrekusha, who carried the Princess out of your garden."

The King gave the gypsy a fat bag of gold coins, and she went away happy. But the King was more angry, even, than before.

"Let my army make ready!" the King gave the order. "We shall march upon Branko and his animal servants. No animals shall get the better of me."

A thousand soldiers were called up. A thousand horses were saddled. A thousand cannon were loaded. Word spread that the King himself would ride at the head of his great army to bring his daughter home.

In Branko's castle, the dog heard the news first. And at once he gathered all the animals together.

"Trouble is on its way," the dog told the others. "The King comes to kill our dear master. Or at best he will take our dear mistress away. We need a great army to protect our master and his bride."

"Yes, we need an army," as usual the animals agreed with the dog.

"Who will fight with us?" The dog looked at them all.

"First the bears! How many bears can you bring to fight on our side?" The dog turned toward Branko's bear servant.

The bear rose up, tall, on his hind legs. He wagged his great head, and he said, "Oh, I can call up a hundred or more."

"How many of your brothers can we count upon, Fox?"

"I can bring here two hundred. Of that I am sure." The fox was determined to outdo the bear.

"How many wolves?"

"Five hundred wolves!" the wolf was determined to outdo the fox.

"And you with the tall ears, how many hares?" the dog asked next.

"Eight hundred, at least!" the hare cried.

"What about you, Mouse? What can you do for our dear master?"

"Three thousand mice will fight on our side in this terrible war," the cocky mouse squeaked.

The mole was not to be beaten. He promised six thousand of his mole tribe.

Only the kumrekusha could not talk in very large numbers.

"There are less than one hundred kumrekushas in all the wide world," said the giant bird. "But every one of them will be ready."

"We shall have a fine army," the dog declared. "I will be its head. From now on call me 'General.'

"Go now, all of you! Call out all your brothers, your cousins and your good friends. We have not very much time!" This was the first order of "General" Dog.

What a sight it must have been to see so many thousands of animals gathered together! When all had arrived at Branko's castle, "General" Dog gave his next orders.

"The first night, when the King's army is asleep in camp, the bears and the wolves will fall upon the horses. The second night the mice will gnaw the straps of their saddles in two. The third night the foxes and hares will eat through their cannon ropes.

"The fourth night the moles will dig ditches in the path of the King's army. Last of all, the kumrekushas will drop stones down upon the heads of the King's men."

This was the plan which "General" Dog had worked out. And it was a good plan.

When the King's men awoke after their first night in camp, they saw a terrible sight. All of their horses had been killed by the wolves and the bears. The King had to send back for a thousand more horses.

Then the next day they found that the mice had eaten their saddle straps in two. They had to ride bareback. That is no way at all for soldiers to gallop into a battle.

After that it was the ropes that pulled their cannon along. The sharp teeth of the foxes and hares had cut these into small pieces.

The soldiers began to be afraid of this strange army of animals. Many wanted to turn around and go home. But the King would not let them. He sent for new saddle straps and new cannon ropes.

Then it was the turn of the six thousand moles. In the dark of the night, they did their work. They ate their way through the earth. They dug giant underground traps. And as quickly as they dug out a pile of earth, the bears and the wolves and the other animals came and carried it off. By morning there was nothing to tell of the deep, deep, deep traps all around the King's camp.

"Hurrah! Hurrah!" the King's men cried that morning. Their horses were safe. Their saddle straps and their cannon ropes were all in one piece.

"The animals have run away," the King shouted joyfully. "We shall run after them. We shall take Branko prisoner. We shall bring my daughter home."

But the King's joy did not last long. His army had only just begun to move, when his men fell, one after the other, into the traps dug by the moles.

At the very same time, the kumrekushas began to drop great stones down upon them. Each giant bird had brought a rock from the mountains in his strong claws. It was as if rocks were raining down on the King's army.

"God Himself is against us," the King cried in dismay. "He rains rocks upon us out of the sky. God, too, is on Branko's side in this war. We cannot fight God in his Heaven and all the animals of the earth, too. We shall go home, and my daughter shall stay here with Branko and her animal friends."

254

No doubt, before long, Branko and his Princess made peace with her father, the King. No doubt the young man took over the kingdom when the old King was gone. If he did, we can be sure Branko ruled the land kindly and well. And we can be sure, too, that, wherever they lived, Branko and his Princess always had a place in their palace for "General" Dog.

It seemed very natural for Frances Carpenter to gather folk tales and myths featuring dogs and cats from all over the world and put them into this book. She has traveled in most of the homelands of her stories, first with her father, later with her diplomat husband. And she has known many remarkable dogs and cats in Washington, where she grew up and now lives, and on the Virginia farm where the family summers. There was a wire-haired terrier who took a cat for walks; a dachshund who could sing; an Irish terrier, the author's constant companion; and Kitty Gray, the cat who played at being a luxurious house pussy in the summer and hunted through the Blue Ridge Mountains all winter. So she knows how *wonderful* dogs and cats can be.